Lewis Woolston grew up in Geraldton, Western Australia. Hating it, he left as soon as he could. He misspent most of his youth in Perth and Adelaide, undertook a short and miserable stint in the Australian Army, and spent years living and working in remote roadhouses on the Nullarbor and in the Northern Territory before settling down. Truth Serum Press published Lewis's first collection *The Last Free Man and Other Stories* (2019), which was shortlisted for Best Fiction in the 2020 Chief Minister's NT Book Awards. He lives in Port Lincoln, South Australia, with his wife and daughter.

REMEMBERING THE DEAD

AND OTHER STORIES

LEWIS WOOLSTON

TRUTH SERUM PRESS

ISBN: 978-1-922427-58-8

BP#00110

Truth Serum Press
32 Meredith Street
Sefton Park SA 5083
Australia

Email: truthserumpress@live.com.au
Website: truthserumpress.net
Truth Serum Press catalogue: truthserumpress.net/catalogue

Cover design © Matt Potter
Cover image *Fremantle, 2002* © Lewis Woolston
Author photograph © Linsey Berryman

Also available as an ePub eBook
ISBN: 978-1-922427-62-5
Also available as a Kindle eBook
ISBN: 978-1-922427-77-9

Truth Serum Press is a member of the
Bequem Publishing collective
bequempublishing.com

In no particular order,
this book is dedicated to:

The City of Fremantle,
for the most fondly remembered and completely
wasted years of my misspent youth;

The City of Adelaide,
for providing a green and pleasant backdrop
to the loneliness and poverty of my twenties; and

The Town of Alice Springs,
for giving me my wife, my daughter
and my first sniff of success.

CONTENTS

THOSE PINE TREES
ACROSS THE STREET

Hush yourself little one, Dad's got you now, there you go, cuddle up to Dad. You make a lot of noise for such a little baby, don't you, now?

What's the time? Where's my phone? It's just gone six-thirty in the morning, well, I suppose I'm getting up early now, aren't I, little one? Your mother and me used to sleep in till ten every Sunday, that's out the window now, isn't it, Chook?

C'mon, we'll get your bottle and we'll sit out on the front porch and let Mum get a bit of sleep. See that sun just coming up? See the way the dawn light hits those pine trees across the street? That's a beautiful morning, almost worth getting woken up for.

I've always loved those big Norfolk Island Pines there across the road. I hope the council never does something stupid like cut them down. Trees like that are a public good, in my opinion.

You finished your sooking, little one? Here, have your bottle. You're lucky you know, you nearly grew up out in the desert where there are no Norfolk Island Pines. Did I ever tell you the story about how me and your mum met up? No, well since you've woken me up and I have nothing better to do while you have your bottle and I watch the dawn rise, I suppose I can tell you the story.

A long time ago little one, I used to be a bit of a drifter. I travelled around the country working in all sorts of odd places. Mining camps, roadhouses, cattle stations, I've done them all, Chook. Free as a bird, I was. I'd do a job for six months or a year and then I'd wander off to the next one. Not a care in the world.

Some of those places, little one, my word, they were rough. Not a place for a little one like you, that's for sure. I remember this one place, a mining camp up in the NT, we had a mouse plague because of all the rain we had that year. Of course, in the bush nothing happens in isolation. When the mice reached huge numbers, the snakes followed. Found a metre and a half long taipan in my bed one morning. I've never moved that fast before or since.

I worked up in the Kimberly for a while, Chook, on a prawn trawler out of Wyndham. Hard work but the things I saw, little one! Crocodiles, sharks, barramundi the size of a full-grown man with flesh that melted like butter when you cooked it. When you get off the bottle and onto solid food I'll get you to try barramundi. Not the crap they serve down here which is probably not even real barra, we'll do a family trip up to the Kimberly one day and get some out of the river. Nothing like it, little one.

Wasn't all good times, Chook, nothing ever is. You won't realize this until you get older, but you can actually die from loneliness and even if you don't die from it, it can make you strange. That's the thing about that sort of life, you're free but

2

nobody is there for you when it counts. I'll tell you something for nothing, little one, if I hadn't met your mother I reckon I'd have gone proper strange permanently. I've seen it happen to other men. It was only meeting your mother that saved me from that fate, I reckon.

Finished your bottle, have you? God, you're getting big now, just hoovering down your food, aren't you? You'll be walking before I know it. Here, sit on my lap, little one and watch the sun come up over those pine trees across the street. See if that magpie is going to give us a morning call.

I remember when I met your mother, she said hello in her Dutch accent and I was sold on her there and then. You know I kissed her for the very first time on a morning just like this, little one? We were both working at a little roadhouse near Tennant Creek, she was a backpacker and I was just a drifter. We'd been up all night with the other staff having too much to drink and just as the sun was coming up we kissed for the first time. No Norfolk Island Pines up there though, just the red dust and scrub.

Six months later we came down south to Port Lincoln, a month later she was pregnant with you and a month after that we were married. I'll no doubt tell you that story again when you're older, more than once probably, but it's a good story. It does me good to remember how close I came to being lost out there forever. It makes me appreciate what I have now. You, my little Chook, and your mum, I'm a lucky man when it's all said and done. I could have very easily spent the rest of my life drifting, another lost soul out in the bush, there's plenty of them.

Instead, I got to have this little family in this little house, across the street from these big old Norfolk Island Pines.

C'mon now Chook, I reckon your nappy needs changing and I think I can hear your mum up and about. Let's get her a cuppa and get you sorted. Those pines will still be there tomorrow.

STUCK AT KULGERA

It had been raining for days, five days to be exact. In the middle of the driest continent on Earth the rain stubbornly refused to stop. Prior to this five-day run they'd had two days of intermittent sunshine and before that four days of solid, pounding rain.

They were cut off.

The Finke and the Palmer had overflowed their banks. Huge areas of the flat red dirt country were under a foot or two of water. The Stuart Highway was underwater in several places and no traffic was driving anywhere.

The staff at Kulgera Roadhouse weren't too put out, really. Most of them were backpackers or other transient types and this was all part of the adventure of roadhouse life. They drank beer and took photos of the water rising dangerously close to the front door of the roadhouse. Then at night they continued on with the absorbing game of roadhouse romance, staff quietly sneaking into each other's rooms to cuddle and copulate. Sometimes life-long bonds were formed, sometimes hearts were broken, sometimes children were conceived or diseases spread. They were young and alive; what did it matter if flood waters cut the highway?

The Truckies were less relaxed about it. They had schedules to keep, deadlines to meet and homes to return to. Every hour, on the hour, they asked for an update on the road from the long-suffering local police. Every hour, on the hour, the long suffering local police officer told them the same thing; the Highway is cut in three places and won't be passable for at least a day even if the rain stopped right now. Bitterly, like the soldiers of a defeated army, they would trudge back to their trucks or the front bar of the roadhouse to discuss what they were going to do. They rang their bosses via sat phone and updated them. There was nothing anyone could do.

The grey nomads in the caravan park were somewhat put out by it all. They had expected sunshine. Kulgera was in the middle of a desert after all, they had expected to only be here a day or so at the very most. It had been a solid week for some of them. The men gathered together to discuss the situation, clustered in a little circle like grey-haired cardigan-wearing penguins. Weather predictions were analysed, previous experiences with floodwater recalled. These serious discussions were of about the same value as reading tea leaves. Their womenfolk gathered amongst themselves but were more bothered by the lack of television reception. *Home and Away* was on tonight, they said, how were they supposed to watch it if this weather kept up? Nobody had an answer.

A solitary young man stayed in his tent on the far side of the caravan park. He'd been travelling alone, living out the back of his old troopy, hoping to get to Kakadu before the season started. He had a job lined up there. Decent pay plus accommodation and meals provided. He worried now that he wasn't going to get there in time. He'd rung the manager and told him he was stuck at Kulgera because of the rain. The manager had assured him he would hold his position for him but he knew from past experience how fickle these people can be. He was desperately hoping the rain would stop soon. He needed this job.

Late in the afternoon, almost at last light, a lone police car crept back into the roadhouse. The two officers, soaked and weary, got out and trudged into the front bar. All eyes were on them right away. The roadhouse manager greeted them and asked what the news was.

'Just stopped raining north of here an hour ago, if it holds, might be able to open the Highway tomorrow arvo, if it holds.'

The entire front bar listened, calculating how long it would take to get where they wanted to go, hoping he was right.

ON GUARD FOR THE MILENNIUM

My wife and I were discussing great moments in history the other night, idly wondering what might happen in the lifetime of our two-year-old daughter. We started recalling the big moments we'd both lived through. The obvious ones like the fall of the Berlin Wall and 9/11 came to mind. Then my wife recalled where she was at the turn of the Millennium and she asked me where I was.

The memory came slowly to my mind and as I told my wife she laughed her head off. "You have to write this down," she insisted and the next morning I thought about it and agreed with her.

So here it is.

I was still in the Army back then. I'd joined up straight from High School to get the fuck away from my Christian fundamentalist parents and the shithole town I grew up in. That was my only reason for joining the Army. I wasn't gung-ho or patriotic, I didn't believe any of the bullshit, it was just a better, or to be more accurate, less worse, option than what I had where I grew up.

I wasn't a very good soldier. In fact, if we're being truthful, I was a shithouse soldier. I hated the discipline, I'm naturally an idle daydreamer and I don't like groups. I was completely unsuitable for the Army really. I'm surprised they took me now that I look back on it but I suppose they must have been short that month.

Anyway, in my time in the Army I got into a bit of trouble for various things and used to get put on punishment details fairly regularly. The Army operates on a very simple discipline theory. You fuck up, they make life unpleasant for you, the more you fuck up the more unpleasant life becomes until you either get with the program or get the boot.

It works most of the time.

I don't remember what I'd done this particular time. Most likely got in late from leave or been still half drunk on morning parade or something like that. Anyway I got given extra guard duty on the front gate of the barracks. Things have changed since then I've been told, apparently they have private security contractors guarding the gates into the bases now. I don't know for sure, that's only what I've heard, I'm not the sort who keeps up with all the Army shit now I'm out.

This was the old Enoggera Barracks in Brisbane. I don't even know if the Army still uses that base anymore. I got assigned guard duty on New Year's Eve 1999 because fuck me and my life, that's why. The Army are experts on inflicting misery, they've got it down to a fine art.

I watched as all the other blokes headed out the gate in their civvy clothes, they all had leave passes and cash in their pockets. Some of the blokes from my platoon passed by on their way out and gave me shit as they went. I was not only prevented from having fun on the biggest night of the year but I was now a joke in my unit. Fuck my life.

I remember it was Sergeant Holt with me that night running the Guard. Sergeant Holt was an old sweat who'd been in the Army for about 16 years at that point. He'd joined during the "big sleep" which is what the old hands called the period between Australia pulling out of Vietnam in 1972 and the East Timor deployment in 1999 when we were a peace time Army. During this time blokes had entire careers without ever going overseas or firing a shot in anger. Blokes like Sergeant Holt joined from shithole country towns and impoverished post-industrial suburbs because the Army was a better option than anything else going at the time. They joined to milk the Australian Taxpayer out of every cent they could and avoid the competitive private sector workplace. They became insti-tutionalised over time and were incapable of fitting back into the real world.

I personally didn't mind the old sweats like Sergeant Holt. They tended to be pragmatic and realistic. So long as you didn't fuck around too much and rock the boat too much they were happy to leave you be. It was the gung-ho fuckwits who made life in the Army unbearable for me. Wannabe heroes who joined with the intention of going to war and winning medals, people who craved glory and excellence, people who believed. I hate cunts like that.

Sergeant Holt and I watched the mad rush of soldiers with leave passes head out the gate and into taxis, all eager to be in Brisbane pissing on when the big countdown came up.

Eventually the rush thinned out and we were left alone at the gatehouse.

'Well, Private I suggest we settle in, I doubt we'll see anyone until nearly sunrise now. Go make us a brew, milk and two for me.'

I did as I was commanded while Holt had his sneaky cigarette just outside the guard house where he knew any passing officer wouldn't be able to see him. He came in once I'd made our brews and pulled out a little radio hidden under old files in a drawer. He plugged it in and tuned it to Triple J. He stretched out in his chair and sipped his brew.

'Right, just make sure you walk back and forth in front of the gate every twenty minutes so you get seen on camera giving a fuck, aside from that just relax young fella, all the action is in town tonight, I doubt there's more than twenty people on the whole base right now.'

I sipped my brew and wandered outside. It was ghostly quiet. The lights from the barracks and offices shone on one side and if I looked towards town I could just see the lights of Brisbane itself. In between them was me, the sorriest cunt of a soldier there ever was, guarding a gate nobody wanted to enter on New Year's Eve 1999. My life had been almost nothing but suffering up to that point and it looked set to continue. The silent gum trees down the length of the road gave no comfort at all.

I stepped inside and saw Holt had settled down into his chair and pulled out a pile of titty magazines and hot rod magazines from somewhere. The Australian Taxpayer was being well served tonight. I sat down in the other chair and listened to the radio. Triple J were making a big deal of the coming Millennium. They had presenters talking, people calling in and requesting songs and an ongoing but light-hearted debate about whether or not the Y2K bug was going to turn out to be a real thing or not.

It was Adam Spencer and Wil Anderson presenting. They took calls and requests from people and I would have enjoyed listening to them if I wasn't stuck where I was on this night of nights. They played some good songs and talked a lot of funny shit and I started to relax a little and be slightly less miserable. Holt listened as well in between thumbing through titty magazines. He liked the harder rock type songs and would tap his feet while he listened, his boot drumming the beat on the grotty carpet of the gatehouse.

Then this weirdo called in. It was a bloke but with a real effeminate voice, he sounded unwell too, like really unwell. One of the presenters, I'm pretty sure it was Adam Spencer, asked him what he was doing for the big night.

'I'm taking it easy, my doctor says I can't go out, I have AIDS and I'm dying, I wanted to live to see Mardi Grais next year but it doesn't seem like I will so I wanted to enjoy New Year's as much as I can.'

The presenter must have thought this was a bit heavy for such a party night and wanted to cut it short, he asked the caller if there was a song they could play for him. The caller, sounding a little more manic and unstable now, refused to be put off that easily. Apparently he had something to say and he was going to say it.

'Look what happened to me was really wrong you know, I was lured into Hyde Park after dark and they tied me up to a tree and raped me, it was very wrong you know, but look, I just want to have a good time for my last New Year's Eve, ok? I want everyone to have a good time, ok? Because life is about having a good time you know and just because something very wrong happened to me doesn't mean we can't all enjoy New Year's Eve but look everyone, please just stay safe, ok? And look ...'

Adam Spencer, apparently feeling this was getting out of hand now, tried to cut him off again. He asked, more insistently this time, if there was a song they could play for him.

'Look it was a terrible thing what happened to me you know, but look, I just hope everyone has a good time tonight and just remember to practise safe sex, ok? And be careful out there because there are dangerous people out there, you know. The people who raped me have never been caught, you know, but look, everyone I just want you to all enjoy New Year's Eve, ok?'

The presenter finally cut him off and played "Disco 2000" by Pulp to cover the awkwardness.

'Fuck they have some weird cunts on Triple J,' was Sergeant Holt's verdict.

I went outside and walked back and forth across the gate making sure I was seen on camera giving a fuck.

We sat around a little longer and it was almost time for the countdown. A thought occurred to Sergeant Holt.

'You reckon this Y2K thing is real or what, Private?'

I shrugged. 'Dunno Sarge, all these computer people are supposed to be geniuses aren't they? Surely they wouldn't miss a little thing like that? Then again, it's always the little things that get you in the end.'

I paused and thought about it.

If all the computers went kaput at midnight and civilization collapsed, would it really be a bad thing? I had no love for civilization. I couldn't see what it had ever done for me. Thanks to the Army, I knew how to survive and fight so on the off chance we started a Mad Max style dystopia at midnight tonight I'd probably come out a winner rather than a casualty. The end of civilization would mean the end of the Army and its bullshit rules, it would mean the end of the jobs/careers/money game that I hated and was no good at. It would be the end of taxes and governments, the end of petty rules and hypocritical standards, the end of everything but the real, natural struggle to survive.

The more I thought about it the more I wanted the Y2K bug to be real.

The clock counted down. The presenters on the radio grew more and more excited. They counted down the last ten seconds.

Then ...

Nothing happened.

Sergeant Holt wished me happy new year and I returned his good wishes. I went outside and walked back and forth across the gate again. There would be no apocalypse. The bullshit would continue indefinitely. I was genuinely disappointed.

The night lagged on miserably. Sergeant Holt got me to make another brew. I took mine outside and stood on the road in front of the gate. There was no traffic anywhere although I could hear a dull hum from the direction of the city. I sipped my coffee and listened to radio coming from the gatehouse, they were playing "Feeding Circle" by Pollyanna, I remember thinking that the future had to be better, it just had to be, life couldn't be unbroken misery and suffering from womb to tomb, could it?

The night wore on.

After about one in the morning the first return taxis started coming back disgorging their cargoes of drunken soldiers in front of the gate. I checked passes and IDs and let them enter.

At about two in the morning one taxi stopped and a soldier basically fell out of the rear passenger door. He then crawled on all fours towards the gatehouse before collapsing two metres short of the gate.

Sergeant Holt was not amused.

'These cunts just go overboard, any reason or no reason at all, they go overboard. He's probably drunk a month's pay tonight. Not a thought in his head about saving for a rainy day.'

He shook his head and searched the man for ID.

'Fuck me he's a Sergeant over in Echo Company. He should know better, the fucking dickhead.'

He shook his head some more and I asked what were we going to do with him?

'I'll show you how to move a drunk idiot, watch this.'

He reached down and put his hands between the man's legs. He gripped his testicles firmly and pulled and twisted at the same time. The man came to with a start and a yell.

'C'mon Sergeant! Get mobile! This shit won't wash!'

Sergeant Holt yelled but with a grin on his face. The drunken man attempted to stand but finding it impossible resumed his drunken crawl into the base. He made it through the gate and crossed the road on all fours onto a lawn area. He got maybe ten metres onto the lawn before he vomited profusely all over his hands and collapsed, face first into his own vomit.

'We'll leave the cunt there, the 2IC of our Battalion does his morning jog across that lawn just before dawn. He'll find him and have his balls.'

This prospect amused Sergeant Holt and he laughed a little. We walked back into the gatehouse.

The night slowly bled into morning. The first hints of sunlight tickled the horizon. Our relief arrived. Sergeant Holt and I headed up towards the mess. We parted company, he went into the Sergeant's Mess and I went into the Private's.

'First breakfast of the Millennium Private, better make it a good one.'

He was cheerful; I was just tired. I sat down and had bacon, eggs and beans with orange juice. My first breakfast of the Millennium. It wasn't so bad.

THE ARMY PENIS WASHING METHOD

When it comes up in conversation and I tell people that I was once in the Army the reaction usually depends on that person's political views.

If they lean to the left of the political spectrum they are cautious and I can see their tiny little minds ticking over wondering if I killed little brown kids in the Middle East. Sometimes, if they are a little braver than their fellows, they will ask me outright if I killed anyone and do I feel ashamed that I served the American-led imperialism?

On the other hand if they are a more conservative-minded person they will often thank me for my service and make patriotic noises. Sometimes they ask if I "got any action" as though a deployment was a bucks' night in the city.

Both groups are of course way off. I never left Australia, never fired my weapon in anger and never gave that much of a shit. The truth about why I was in the Army is both less noble and less monstrous than these people imagine.

I was young and I needed the money.

Or more accurately I was young and desperately wanted to escape the shitty little town I grew up in and my religious fundamentalist parents. I grew up in a place called Geraldton on the coast of WA. Back then, before the mining boom, it was a total backwater populated by dropkicks and bogans. The prospects for young people growing up there were grim. I personally knew of people who finished High School on a Friday and signed up for the dole on Monday. It was that sort of place.

Now add in being raised by religious parents who were enthusiastic about the apocalypse and abhorred all forms of fun and maybe you can understand why the bullshit of the Army recruitment people who came to my school sounded good to me.

One of the things you should understand is that people like me, coming from towns like mine and situations like mine, make up the bulk of Army general enlistment recruiting. Every white trash shithole with high unemployment is well represented in the Army. Places like Shepparton, Geelong, Dubbo, Toowoomba and Launceston are fertile grounds for the recruitment people. Because if you're young and growing up in these places the Army seems like a good deal. Sure, you get shouted at, subjected to discipline and you might get your dumb arse sent to the Middle East but that's still better than working at Hungry Jack's in Shepparton or being on the dole in Dubbo or filling shelves at the Coles in Toowoomba or in my case living with religious parents in Geraldton.

The Army might seem awful to a lot of people but awful is a relative thing.

For me, the worst part of becoming a soldier was the almost total dehumanisation. You are no longer a person, you are a number, a rank, a uniform. Once you sign the papers and do the oath you are property of the Australian Government and therefore disposable.

You are moved around like a piece of equipment. Shifted here and there like a truck, except that the trucks are a lot more valuable and cared for than you.

Which is not to say that you aren't looked after in a fashion. You are Government property and they maintain you so that you're fit for purpose. The food is actually really good. The health care is great although I was a bit worried about the amount of vaccinations we got. In the 12 weeks of basic training I received 32 injections and was only told what three or four of them were. I'm sure it's nothing to worry about. I'm sure the Government wouldn't do weird experiments on us without telling us. Would they?

The most dehumanising thing I experienced by far was the Army penis washing method.

We were assembled up before the showers. The female recruits got taken into their showers with a female Corporal; more about that later.

Us boys were divided up into "cut" and "uncut" groups for obvious reasons. Each group was assigned a Corporal and taken into the showers. Now the Army has a very specific teaching method, explain, demonstrate and repeat, they use this method for everything. It's how they turn knuckle-dragging bogans into perfectly fine soldiers. It's always the same method of teaching regardless of what you're learning. From stripping and cleaning your rifle to washing your penis, doesn't matter.

We were shown the correct, Army approved way of washing our penis. The Corporal instructing us peppered his demonstration with colourful phrases such as 'make sure you get the cheese out, I'll have no cheese merchants in this platoon' and 'polish under the helmet and make him clean, every solider should have a polished helmet.' I found it a little disconcerting. Judging from the looks on the other recruits' faces they did too.

We were barked at to get to it and we reluctantly did. The Corporal paced up and down the length of the showers barking instructions and admonishing recruits for poor technique. He stopped at the bloke next to me and barked, 'Do you work for Kraft, recruit?' The lad was dumbfounded and didn't know what to say. 'Because the last time I saw that much cheese was at the Kraft factory, now get in there with the soap, you useless fuck!'

Not for the first or the last time I thought to myself, 'This bullshit wasn't in the recruitment videos.'

Eventually after much embarrassment and scrubbing, we were deemed clean enough to pass muster. We were allowed to dry off and put our uniforms back on. Young lads that we were, we got over the awkwardness and embarrassment of it all by talking shit, making jokes and teasing each other. By the time we were walking out of the shower our morale was more or less back to normal.

The girl recruits were coming out of their showers about the same time. They had an expression on their faces similar to what you'd see on someone who's just seen a kitten set on fire. Shock and horror.

They refused to speak about what they'd seen or been taught by their female Corporal. To this day I have never been able to find out what they learnt. Probably for the best.

THE DISAPPOINTED SOLDIER

The Army recruitment people are the biggest liars I've ever personally encountered. They tell lies that would make a used car salesman blush. The things they promise you to make you sign on the dotted line are worth nothing once you get on that bus to basic training.

I did the tests and they discovered I was partially colour blind. Red-green deficiency, they called it. It meant there was a big list of things I couldn't do in the Army. They showed me the list of what I could do and I was leaning towards the Transport Corps, four-year sign up, come out as a qualified truck driver, didn't seem too bad to me. The recruitment guy tried to talk me into joining as a medic instead.

'I dunno, that's a six-year sign up, seems a bit much,' I said.

'You'll be almost a doctor when you get out, the world will open right up for you, isn't it worth six years to get that sort of training and opportunities?'

Seventeen-year-old idiot that I was, I believed him. Turned out "almost a doctor" amounted to being the first aid guy in a company. It sucked arse and it lasted for six long years.

After I'd done my basic training and my medic training I was based in Brisbane and spent most of my time at the Regimental Aid Post on base. My commanding officer was a grumpy arsehole called Captain Pascoe. He was one of those men you come across who is bitterly disappointed with how their life has turned out and intend to take it out on anyone they come across who can't return the hostility. Waitresses, taxi drivers, underlings at work: it doesn't matter, they will feel every drop of the bitter disappointment he lives with every day.

I hate arseholes like that.

I kept my head down and worked out a way to stay in his good books.

I discovered the reason for Captain Pascoe's disappointment with life. He was a failed war hero. He was descended from a line of men who'd won glory in wars, a father who'd been in Vietnam and Malaya and distinguished himself, a grandfather who'd been a hero of the Kokoda Trail and a great-grandfather who had won medals in the trenches of the Western Front in the First World War.

Captain Pascoe had grown up determined to do the same but alas, fate is not kind to everyone. He also had partial colour blindness, red-green deficiency like me, and thus couldn't join the infantry. Even worse for his dreams he came of age during the "big sleep", the gap between Vietnam ending in 1972 and the Timor Deployment in 1999 when the Australian Army did basically nothing. He was destined to serve in a peace time military, no deployments, no wars, no chance for bravery and glory, just the mind-numbing routine of barracks life and exercises and constant cost cutting by the government.

Coming as I did from a poor white trash shithole town I resented his ingratitude for what life had given him. The Army had trained him as a Doctor, he could've left after his time was up and entered the private sector, made a good living and lived a comfortable upper-middle-class lifestyle. I know I would have taken that route if I'd had the opportunity. But no, Captain Pascoe wanted to be a war hero, and the more that ambition faded from possibility with every passing year, the bitterer he became.

He discovered early on that I was quite the reader, I was a slacker and every opportunity I could get I would hide away and read or snooze. He realized I knew a thing or two about military history from my reading and enjoyed quizzing me.

'Quick Woolston, who commanded British Forces in Burma 1942-1945?'

'General William Slim, sir, arguably the best British General of the War and the least praised by history.'

'Correct Woolston, now get back to work.'

He'd do this at random times throughout the day, fire off a question and try to catch me out not knowing something. I was pretty good at it and was rarely caught out. We both enjoyed it and it helped to break up the monotony of the day.

I found a reference to his grandfather in a book about the Kokoda campaign and told him about it. I went up in his estimation from then on and he waxed lyrical about what his grandfather had done in the War and what a hero he'd been. I knew then that I'd found his weakness, this daydreaming of glory and frustration with the dismal reality of life in a peace time Army. I cynically but carefully played up to him, listening to his stories about his long line of heroic ancestors, being interested in the same things he was interested in. Pretty soon I was the golden boy in our little section and had privileges and was able to slack off with impunity.

Captain Pascoe was a rabid misogynist and hated the fact that women were allowed in the Army now. He grouped all female soldiers into two groups: "bushpigs" and "dykes", and he despised them both.

In a peace time Army the medical staff end up dealing with a lot of sexually transmitted diseases. Soldiers get leave, they go into town and get drunk and fuck anything with a hole and a pulse. Some time later they present to the RAP with a nasty rash or something more serious. Dealing with all this is tedious, unpleasant work and nobody enjoys it. Captain Pascoe enjoyed it even less than most. I could almost see the thoughts forming in his head, a grandfather who'd help save Australia from Japanese invasion on the Kokoda Trail, a great-grandfather who'd been decorated in the trenches of the First World War, and here he was, putting ointment on the manky penis of an infantry grunt who'd fucked some skank on leave and was suffering the consequences.

One of the methods the Army Medical people use to try to track and prevent the spread of STDs is what's called a "clap map", which is basically a big diagram on the wall listing who caught what, when they caught it and what particular strain the nasty was. You can use this to track who has been fucking who and where the nasty came from in the first place.

A complicating factor is the Army has strict rules governing relationships between personnel. If you fuck the wrong person and they can prove it then you can be punished and maybe even discharged. Captain Pascoe made it his mission to get as many female soldiers discharged as possible. He used the clap map to prove they'd been fucking someone they shouldn't have and get their arses booted out of the Army. Another way he took his petty revenge on life for not allowing him to be a war hero.

I remember one particular strain of nasty that went through the barracks while I was there. Multiple infantry grunts were coming in with a disgusting rash right on the head of their penis. Captain Pascoe took samples, treated them and documented it all on the clap map. The problem was that no female soldiers were showing up with the same strain of nasty. I ventured my opinion that the Infantry grunts must be catching it off base.

'Don't talk shit, Woolston, these boys are from different units, they've had leave at different times, but they all turn up with the same strain of nasty, no way this is an off base nasty. We have a dirty bushpig on this base and I'm going to find her.'

He kept at it for a week or two, determined to find his bushpig so he could have her punished.

Sure enough, a week or two later a female solider from the stores presented at the RAP with what the nurse privately referred to as "the most battered and diseased vagina I've ever seen." Samples were taken, treatments issued, Captain Pascoe was happy as only those who hate life can be. The poor soldier was charged with conduct breaches and disciplined severely, word got around the barracks and she copped a lot of comments from people. Eventually, after a half-arsed suicide attempt, she was discharged from the Army.

I served out my time in the army and hated every minute of it. I got out and never looked back. People often find it hard to believe I was ever in. I lack the discipline and martial bearing they expect from an ex-soldier. Truth is, I was never a soldier. I was a poor kid who joined the Army out of desperation and managed to serve out my time. Nothing more.

I never heard of Captain Pascoe again. He probably did get the deployment he wanted eventually, after Timor kicked off in 1999 the Australian Army was deployed to the Solomon Islands, Iraq and Afghanistan; nearly everyone got a tour somewhere. I never saw his name on any casualty lists and I never saw his name on the lists of medals and awards so I gather he remained undistinguished and frustrated. He'd be retired now. I expect he's sitting at the bar of some golf course somewhere on the north coast of New South Wales talking shit with the other old blokes and drinking too much, getting fat and old, and closer to the grave like we all do.

A disappointed soldier till the end.

OLD MATE AT THE BOTTLE SHOP

There was something about Sunday arvos, Tony thought, even when you had to work it felt different, more relaxed somehow. The customers were more easy-going, and you could almost call being at work fun and enjoyable. The bottle shop hummed along, everyone content to be there.

Tony knocked off at four-thirty, just as the shadows were growing long and the arvo was threatening to turn into evening proper. He walked down to his car and debated stopping off at the fish and chip shop on the way home. He was parked a little way from the pub and the bottle shop, all the spots had been taken when he got to work, and in the gathering evening he walked oblivious to what was around him. Bugger it, he thought, I'll get fish and chips on the way home.

He never saw or heard the man come behind him as he fumbled with his keys. The blow that knocked him down was silent and sudden. All he was aware of was an explosion of pain in the base of his skull and the dirty surface of the car park suddenly on his face.

'Remember me, cunt!'

An angry voice above him, he struggled to focus on the face and tried to say that he did not in fact remember him but a boot in his testicles robbed him of the power of speech. Tony was genuinely baffled as to why he had been attacked although the pain and shock was making it hard to think.

'Maybe you remember my sister, you fucking rock spider!'

Ah, Tony thought, that's what this was about.

'Thought you'd be safe up here in Alice Springs, aye? You thought we'd just forget about it, cunt? Well, I don't forget!'

Several more savage kicks to Tony's ribs reinforced this last point.

Tony should have known. He'd thought it was all over. He'd done eleven years in prison back in Victoria, then two more years on parole unable to leave the state or go out after dark, registering his every movement with the Police.

As soon as parole had ended he'd left Victoria and come to the Northern Territory and settled in Alice Springs. He'd been told in prison by some of the older repeat offenders that this was a good place to hide out, that people up here didn't ask too many questions, that your criminal record in Victoria wouldn't mean anything up here. It wasn't entirely true, he'd found, but it was mostly true, people didn't ask too many questions, employers rarely asked for a police clearance unless it was a Government job or it involved kids. He'd got his current job at the bottle shop after a ten-minute chat with the boss. Easy as that.

He'd hoped the past could be forgotten.

Now it seemed the past had tracked him down.

The angry young man had mounted him and was raining blows on his head, shouting in his face, foam and spittle spewing from his mouth, years of built up anger and pain bursting to the surface. Tony wasn't resisting. The pain was too great and he was too tired. Let him kill me, he thought, it doesn't matter anymore.

Tony woke up under the glare of a Fluro light. The hospital, he thought, I'm in the hospital. So that means I didn't die.

A nurse was speaking to him. He focused on her face to absorb her words.

'You've been assaulted and you have some serious fractures in your skull so we're going to have to keep you here for a couple of days, ok?'

He gave a slight nod, sending a spasm of pain through his body that made him wince. The nurse adjusted his drip, increasing the dose and he felt a warm morphine glow ease through his system. The pain faded away. He slept.

When he woke again a different nurse was asking him if he wanted to talk to the Police. He didn't really want to but he mumbled an okay in response. A Constable walked in. He looked young to Tony's eyes; this fellow was probably in high school when I was doing my prison time, he thought.

'Can you tell us anything about the assault? Did you see the person who assaulted you? Is there any reason why someone might want to harm you?'

Tony pondered his answer for a second. If he told the truth his life here in Alice Springs was over. He'd have to move again. Nobody would tolerate his presence if they knew what he was and what he'd done. Where could he go? If the Northern Territory was no longer safe for him then what remained? Maybe in the North West of Western Australia or the top of Queensland he might be able to find a refuge but it was not ideal. No, he decided, his life was here in Alice Springs, where he could build something free of the past.

But was he free of the past?

Would the angry young man come back?

He'd got blood, put me in hospital, he thought, surely that would satisfy him? What else could he do? Kill me? He tried to think like his pursuer. He doubted this young man wanted to spend years in prison; he probably had a life of his own, maybe a missus and kids. No, he wanted blood and the satisfaction of revenge, things he undeniably had got today.

So would the angry young man now head back to Victoria? Maybe tell his sister that the beast from all those years ago had finally been slain, that justice had been done? Would that satisfy him?

Tony knew that his only real option was to gamble on him being satisfied. In which case he knew what he had to tell the Police.

'Look officer, I didn't really see anything and I don't know why anyone would want to attack me. I'm just old mate at the bottle shop, you know?'

OLD RIVER TREES

The fire fighters were there first, gingerly navigating their way down the dry banks of the Todd River with their flashing lights.

They unrolled their hoses and started spraying the flaming, smoking, gnarled old giant of the river. A River Gum, probably older than the town itself, burning up because some shitbag kid had thought it funny to set it on fire. The smoke had made the dry riverbed temporarily uninhabitable, the local indigenous crew who slept there most of the time had to retreat to the nearby park for the time being, and a motley crowd of them stood now with their blankets and meagre possessions watching the fire fighters work.

The hoses blasted water onto the flame which sizzled and spat as it fought its own extinction. Smoke and steam hissed from the mighty, ancient trunk and the hoses worked back and forth across it.

Once the flame was extinguished, a senior fire fighter inspected the tree.

'It's fucked!' he pronounced.

'Completely fucked!' he expanded.

'Anyone silly enough to be under that tree is likely to have it fall on their heads at any moment. Won't take much more than a stiff breeze to knock down some of those bigger branches.'

He took his phone out and advised Alice Springs Town Council of these facts. He reminded them of the likely legal consequences if they didn't fence off the area and someone was hurt. To ensure his point was understood, he pointed out how many lawyers and activists there were in this town who would take up the cause for some poor indigenous bloke crushed by a burning tree in the river.

The Council took that very seriously. Men from the works depot were redirected from their regular tasks and sent down to the river with temporary fencing, bollards and tape. Very soon a gathering of Council utes and men in hi-vis shirts was parked on the riverbank looking at the smouldering tree in the middle of the dry riverbed.

'This is a bit of a joke,' muttered one Council Worker, who was still nursing a hangover and wanted nothing to do with anything that looked like hard work.

Another bloke spoke loudly and angrily.

'It's these bloody young kids with no respect for anything. They run around doing what they like and the do-gooders make excuses for them. What they need is a bloody good hiding to wake them up to themselves.'

The other council workers muttered agreement.

They slowly, and with much complaining, started to put up the temporary fencing around the charred corpse of the ancient River Gum. The smoke started to dissipate and the River Dwellers began to shuffle back from where they had retreated. As was their habit they called the Council Workers "Council Mob" as if it was their Christian name. They wanted to know if they could set their camp up again.

'Hey, Council Mob, we can camp here again? Us mob been living here all the time but the tree burning and too much smoke but now we back, alright?'

The leading hand amongst the Council Workers shook his head and tried to explain the situation to them.

'Nah Bloke, this tree is dangerous, all burnt out, might fall down anytime, if you're sleeping down here when it falls you might get hurt. Better to go camp over the other side of the River, ok?'

Mutual misunderstanding between the white Council Workers and black River Dwellers was not abated by this conversation. The indigenous man who'd spoken first gave no sign of understanding the points raised by the Council Worker.

'We camp here Council Mob, this is good place, we live here a long time, all us mob.'

With that the Indigenous folk started setting up camp within five feet of the temporary fencing that was supposed to keep everyone away from the burnt-out, dangerous, fire-ravaged old River Gum.

The Council Workers were a little bemused by the casual disregard for safety but didn't see what they could do about it. They had been told to fence off the burnt-out tree, they had done so, and if these people wanted to camp right next to a dangerous place, well, they had been warned and that was that. The leading hand thought about arguing with them but decided against it. He was on record as giving a fuck; whatever would be, would be.

The Council Workers trudged back to their utes on the Riverbank and headed off slowly, not eager to get back to their usual jobs. The leading hand looked back at the smouldering old River Gum still standing in the centre of the dry riverbed. It looked noble, majestic almost, like an ancient statue of a Roman Emperor. A tree like that would have to be a hundred years old, probably more. It seemed a shame for it to be destroyed in one afternoon by a random act of senseless vandalism.

The River Dwellers were settling in, setting down their blankets and bags of meagre possessions. They had been here a long time, they'd seen trees grow and die before and would again. The river wasn't going anywhere.

LIFE MEANS LIFE

I had a job as a prison officer in the Alice Springs Prison for a while a few years back. It was a pretty good wicket and sometimes I think I was a fool to leave but I've learnt in life that it's best to keep moving forward to the next thing rather than try and return to imagined better days of the past.

It was by far the most cynical job I've ever had. By that I mean it would be impossible for anyone with strong ideals and a compassionate nature to do the job for any length of time without going nuts. You had to not give a fuck and the less you gave a fuck the better you were at the job. They reflected this in the recruiting. Anyone who said in the interview they wanted to make a difference and change lives were quietly blacklisted. Dudes who were like "I've got a wife and kids to support and I just desperately need a steady job" were exactly what they wanted.

I'd been working private security in Adelaide for years and was broke, miserable and desperate to get out of my rut. I said so in my interview, so they gave me the job.

After the training course we started work and discovered just how much money there was to be made in overtime. The place was drastically short staffed, people were always leaving, nobody wants to live in Alice Springs and even fewer people want to work in the Alice Springs Prison, so recruitment couldn't keep pace with the number of people quitting.

So if you wanted to, you could clean up on the overtime and make serious money. Some of these overtime shifts were in the Prison itself but many of them were at the hospital in town where prisoners were taken for treatment more serious than what the Prison Clinic could provide. Often the prisoner would be handcuffed to his hospital bed so there was no risk of him getting away. You'd park your arse in a chair outside the room and read a book while raking in that sweet overtime cash.

There was one prisoner we had, he'd been doing a long stretch for raping a young girl out in one of the Aboriginal communities. He was diagnosed with terminal cancer and given 9 to 12 months to live. Thing was, he still had three years left on his sentence.

Now this fellow was classified as a protection prisoner which meant he had to have two officers on him while he was in the hospital. Apparently he was part of one large Aboriginal family group and the girl he'd raped was part of a different group. Now the way they do things out bush involves payback and revenge so we were legally obliged to keep the bastard safe while he was in our custody. I personally thought it was stupid, I mean, if I'm on this guy at the hospital and 20 or 30 angry blackfellas from the girl's family rock up wanting to kill him what are me and one other prison officer going to do about it? Stand aside and let them get on with it, that's what we'd do. I'll be fucked if I get myself hurt defending the life of a child rapist. Let nature take its course, I say.

The news about this bloke's diagnosis and his protection status passed around the prison very quickly. Without exception the reaction of the prison officers was along the lines of, "Sweet, I can do enough overtime to pay for my holiday/new car/new motorbike." This child rapist dying of cancer was seen as a source of overtime, of extra income and nothing more. Like I said, this was the wrong job for anyone who gave a fuck.

My first overtime shift on him was on a Sunday, so it was doubly lucrative. I sat there and read "A Canticle for Leibowitz" while the hours ticked over, each hour representing a solid chunk of overtime cash. The prisoner was unconscious as far as I could tell, handcuffed to the bed, doped up by the doctor to help with the pain; an object, not a person. The nurse checked in on him, I looked up from my book when the nurse walked in, looked up again when she walked out, and the day continued.

Old Terry relieved me that day when my shift was at an end. He had been in the job a long time and was nearing retirement. The thought of it consumed him, it was all he ever talked about, what he was going to do with his retirement, where he was going to live, how much fishing he was going to do. Give him half a chance and he'd tell you all about it.

He'd bought a house down at Bremer Bay on the south coast of WA and was planning to move there and spend the rest of his days in serenity. He just needed that little bit extra cash to set things up. Hence why he was doing this overtime shift on the cancer-ridden child rapist.

'How's Sleeping Beauty today?' he asked when he arrived.

'Vegetated far as I can tell, Terry, he hasn't stirred any.'

Terry put his head around the door and looked in the room at our prisoner. It was just as I'd said, he was cuffed to the bed, had tubes in him and was out to it. No sign that he knew where he was at all.

'This worries me, young fella,' Terry mused. 'Could mean the cunt's not far off dying, I was hoping for plenty more OT, got my eye on a new boat for when I retire.'

I sympathised and repeated what I'd heard from the doctors that our prisoner had a few months more to live.

'Hope so, I want this boat bad, you should see it, aye, got all the mod cons, esky and all that. It's gonna be doing a lot of fishing once I retire down Bremer Bay, mate. Can't fucking wait!'

Terry settled into the chair I'd vacated and pulled out some fishing and boating magazines. Counting down the hours of overtime and the months left until retirement.

DROVE HIM TO IT

They were called the Sally Mahomet Apartments, an ugly block of Housing Commission flats on the corner of Spearwood Road and Peuce Place in Sadadeen, one of the rougher parts of Alice Springs. Nobody who lived there could have told you who Sally Mahomet was and why she deserved a block of flats to her name, but the name was written in large letters, visible from the road, on the side of the building, and that was that. The local police knew the flats and their residents very well, often a radio call would just say "at Sally's" and no further directions were needed.

In the area there were private houses and units and these people resented the flats and their residents for bringing down the tone of the area. These people learned to be very security conscious, locking everything and checking it twice before leaving the house.

In one house, just across from the Sally Mahomets, lived a young man named Derek and his wife. They were new parents; their daughter was all of four months old. They weren't locals, they weren't from Alice Springs or even the NT originally. Few white people are. They had moved here for work; the simple fact was that Derek could get a better job here than he could down south. The only problem was that he had to live here for that job.

Derek and his wife were sitting in their lounge room when they heard her screaming. A guttural howl was coming from the street outside from the direction of the Sally Mahomet Apartments. Derek looked at his wife as she was nursing their daughter. He mentally ran through his options as the howling grew louder and closer. He could continue to ignore it and hope for the best, or he could go out and investigate taking the risks that would result from that choice.

His wife looked up at him.

'That sounds like a woman screaming.'

He nodded and said nothing, not willing to commit himself just yet.

'You should go see what's going on, she might have been bashed or raped or something.'

He sighed and stood up.

He locked the door behind him. Peering into the poorly lit street he saw the woman causing the noise. She had not seen him yet and set off on another bout of fresh wailing.

'HELP ME!!! SOMEBODY HELP MEEEE!!! MY HUS-BAND!!!'

Derek wondered how such a small thin woman could achieve such ear-splitting volume. He walked out towards her and tried to sound like he was in charge of the situation.

'What's going on? What's all the racket about?' he said in his best police officer's voice.

She turned and howled at him.

'MY HUSBAND! HE HUNG HIMSELF! HELP MEEE!!!'

'Show me where he is!' he barked. She led him, still howling, to a tree in the courtyard of the Sally Mahomet Flats.

Sure enough there he was a belt tied and twisted around a branch of the tree. His feet were only inches off the ground but it was enough to get the job done. The man wasn't much to look at. Skinny, scruffy, Aboriginal just like his wife, his sneakers looked newish as they dangled off the ground but aside from that his clothes looked ragged.

For a second Derek thought he should try and lift the man, maybe try and untie the belt from the tree. Then he noticed the thin stream of urine dripping down the man's jeans leg. That meant it was too late. He didn't want some random bloke's death piss on him either.

He did the only practical thing he could think to do. He called the police.

'Yeah I'm at the Sally Mahomet Apartments on Spearwood Road ...'

'What's happening at Sally's?'

'Well, this bloke has hung himself.'

'Ok and who is making all that noise in the background?'

'That's his wife.'

'Police and Ambulance are on their way.'

They were as good as their word. A paddy wagon and an ambulance were there in minutes. Derek felt relieved that the situation was no longer his responsibility. He began to inch away from the scene, hoping to go home to his wife without further drama.

Residents of the flats had come outside for a look now. They were upset and angry and most of them had interrupted their drinking to come outside.

'She drove him to it!' they proclaimed, pointing fingers at the sobbing woman.

One old girl in a cardigan, half pissed, emerged from one of the upstairs flats.

'She was slutting around on him while he was jail, fucking every bloke in town, whitefellas and everything while he was locked up. He found out when he got out of prison that his woman is a slut! That's why he hung himself.'

The rest of the crowd agreed and started piping up with their accusations.

'She done the dirty on him while he was locked up, the slut!' one man shouted.

'She's been a massive slut all over town, everybody knows about it, that's why he hung himself!' a woman's voice loudly accused out of the dark.

The police officer decided enough was enough.

'You lot go back home, we're sorting this out now.'

The angry crowd showed no sign of listening to him and one or two of them started inching towards the woman. The constable didn't like the look of the situation and called on his radio for back up. Derek slipped away and returned home.

His wife was still holding their daughter as he slipped through the front door. He locked it behind him. She looked up and smiled.

'Was she okay?'

'Yeah, just drunken fighting with her man, you know what these people are like.'

He settled back in next to her on the couch and put his arm around her.

PERMANENT SUNDAY

A small complex of units on the south side of Alice Springs. Besser block rental boxes all in rows. The relentless heat bakes the Besser block walls and makes the concrete deadly to walk on.

Inside the little boxes live people, transient workers who've come to town for a job they couldn't get down south. Most of them don't really want to be here but with the economy in their home states being what it is, they have limited choices. They work and save money, hoping that one day, in six months or a year or two years, they can return home cashed up and successful.

In the meantime, they have to make do with Alice Springs, a town they would never otherwise have set foot in. So they make do with this little block of units built like Army barracks and with about as much charm.

In one unit lives a man who turned thirty a month ago. He is not happy about his age. Just last week he saw the first signs of a receding hairline in the mirror. It wasn't much but it was there. It shits him to tears.

He wakes up this Sunday morning and it's already hot. He turns the air conditioner on and thinks that the electricity bill can go fuck itself. He drinks down two glasses of water in quick succession, hydrating himself, then he switches on the kettle because although it's hot he can't function without a coffee first.

While he's waiting for it to boil he opens the front door and looks outside. The sun is already glaring off the concrete making him squint. There is nobody moving around, nobody doing anything; it's too damn hot. A solitary ring-necked parrot flies past, barely making a sound as it flits between the shelter of two trees.

He shuts the door and pours his coffee and flicks on the TV, more out of habit than any real desire to watch the damn thing. This early on a Sunday morning he has a choice between news, kids cartoons and some fishing show. He chooses the fishing show.

He lets the first hour or so of the day roll past in this fashion. Sips his coffee, vaguely watches the fishing show, thinks about maybe, possibly, potentially doing something with the day, sips his coffee again and seeps into the couch.

He makes some breakfast eventually. While he's doing that he notices how much beer he still has in the fridge, at least half a carton of Crown Lager stubbies. He stops, he could write the day off in a pleasant haze of beer if he wants; nobody is there to stop him.

His phone buzzes and he sees his girlfriend has messaged him. *What you doing today?* she asks, and he has to pause for a moment and think about what he actually is doing today.

Not much, probably going to hit the pool for a couple hours, want to join me? His response is loose, careless and he already knows she's going to say yes. She messages him back, saying she'll be there in twenty minutes.

He lies on the couch and stares at the ceiling while he waits for her to arrive. It's too hot to be enthusiastic about Renee coming over. For a minute he actually toys with the idea of telling her not to come over, he thinks about going back to bed and trying to sleep away Sunday.

Renee arrives, she kisses him at the doorstep and he opens the door for her. She is noisy, telling him about her friend who has just gone through a breakup and then had a minor car accident. He doesn't give a shit but nods and makes appropriate noises at roughly appropriate times.

They settle down on the couch while she finishes her story. When he thinks she's safely done he asks if she brought her bathers with her.

'I keep a pair at your place.'

He looks surprised. She leads him to the wardrobe in his bedroom and shows him.

'Don't you remember me putting all this stuff here?' She swings the wardrobe doors open to reveal a stash of women's clothes. Shorts, jeans, underwear and a one piece swimsuit, white with pink lines up the side, all piled up ready to go. He realises they are a lot further along in this relationship than he thought.

'Oh, okay then, makes sense I suppose.' He tries to keep the shock and worry out of his voice. She really is starting to nest, he thinks to himself, this is getting really serious.

They change, grab towels and head down to the pool. The unit complex has a small pool for the use of residents. It's fenced off and theoretically the gate is locked all the time, but they often have to chase out ratbag kids who aren't supposed to be there.

This morning it's quiet, the entire complex of units is asleep, probably everyone has decided it's too damn hot to do anything. They have the pool to themselves. They slide in slowly, afraid to break the silence, the cold water soothing their skin while the chlorine stings their noses.

They embrace in the middle of the pool, feet tippy-toeing on the bottom as they hold each other and kiss gently. Life is good right in this moment.

They swim and potter around for another hour or so. The bloke who lives in the unit two doors up has his kids this weekend. They hear them before they see them. The kids are excited and noisy, so they're not sticking around. As they exit through the pool gate the harassed dad is telling his kids to be careful.

'Slow down you kids, you'll go arse up if you're not careful and then there'll be tears.'

The children run and scream, utterly ignoring his warnings.

They walk back to the unit hand in hand. Renee looks for something for lunch. He sees her arse as she bends over. She's always had a great arse, he thinks and he reaches out for a playful grab.

She jumps a little and giggles; he tries for more. She laughs and soon enough they have abandoned the kitchen for the bedroom.

Afterwards they lie together, no sheet covering them, air conditioner blasting, covered in sweat. Her bathers are on the floor next to his board shorts. They are in no hurry to continue the day. Only hunger motivates them to move.

Renee chucks on a pair of her shorts and his old Metallica t-shirt before heading out to the kitchen.

'How about salami and cheese toasties for lunch?' she calls out to him.

'Sounds good' he replies.

He reluctantly puts some clothes on and gets moving. He flicks through the TV channels. There is nothing but shit on. He looks at the ramshackle pile of DVDs in the corner.

'Want to watch one of the Marvel movies again?' he asks.

'I'm not bothered' she answers.

They settle in on the couch with their toasties and gaze at a movie they've both seen already.

'So, have you been looking on the job websites for something down south?'

He sighs. He knew this topic wasn't over and done with yet.

'Yeah, I had a look the other day.'

'And?'

'There's still fuck all going anywhere down south, we're better off staying up here.'

She sighs. This isn't the end of the conversation.

'You've been here nearly two years, your job's paid for you to get a couple tickets that you can use down south, it's time you took the next step, babe. Do you want to be stuck in Alice Springs forever?'

'I'm on a good gig here, babe. My boss is good, my job pays more than I would get down south, life is easy up here, why throw away a cruisy life just to go back to the rat race?'

She sits up rigid.

'That's how you intend to go through life, isn't it? Always looking for the cruisy option! You'll spend your whole life in this place because it's easy, you'd rather be relaxed in a shithole than put a bit of effort into life down south. That's it, isn't it?'

That is exactly it but he daren't say it to her face.

'C'mon Renee, it's Sunday, we're having a nice day, I have to go back to work at sparrow's fart tomorrow morning, let's not argue and ruin our Sunday.'

'Sunday! It's always fucking Sunday for you! Permanent Sunday! That's your life, one long Sunday arvo doing fuck all and thinking, she'll be right, mate! Meanwhile, there's stuff happening down south, in the cities and it's just passing you by. Oh, but don't worry, it's Sunday arvo, have another beer and sit by the pool while the world goes past. You and all the other dropkicks in this town!'

She storms off to the bedroom. He thinks she might be crying. Reluctantly he turns off the movie and follows her. Lying down next to her on the bed, he puts his arm around her gently and tries to comfort her.

'C'mon now, there's no need for this, we're ok you and me, why make a fuss about what might or might not happen in the future? We probably will go back down south at some point, there's no need to rush these things. The city will still be there in a year or two. Why get all upset about it?'

She's silent for a minute. Is he convincing her? He hears her sniffle gently.

'I can't spend all my life up here, babe, I just can't. Promise me you'll keep looking at the job websites, won't you? Something is bound to come up that you can do, promise me?'

'Of course, I'll keep looking. It's just that good jobs are rarer in the city and there's a lot more competition. Sooner or later something will come up, it's just going to take a little while. In the meantime, we should just enjoy life up here. C'mon, it's Sunday, let's not fight. Let's get a couple of beers and go back down the pool for the arvo. Maybe we can get a feed of Indian for dinner tonight? C'mon, life isn't that bad.'

She softens in his arms. They hold each other. Her complaints are growing more frequent and more intense. Things are going to come to a head sooner or later. Either he gives in to her and they make the move back to the city or he tells her to fuck off. He thinks for a moment and can't decide which option he prefers. Neither really. He'd prefer if things stayed the way they are indefinitely. Just one long Sunday afternoon.

THE GIRL IN THE GREEN PAISLEY DRESS

The amount of stuff you see as a council worker around town is quite remarkable. I've often thought it's worth a book in its own right.

For some reason, despite wearing hi-vis clothes and driving a ute with a dirty great council logo on the side, you seem to blend into the background and people regularly fail to notice you. Instead they continue with whatever they were doing and that is often horrifying or hilarious or tragic. It's the luck of the draw what you get.

My offsider and I were working on the hospital lawns one day and the life around us continued as if we weren't there. The hospital lawns function as a big open-air social centre for the street people of Alice Springs. Black or white, local or blow-in, they all congregate here to make friends, buy and sell drugs, fight and fuck and sometimes just sleep under a shady tree. It's their spot and everyone knows it.

As we worked and picked up the rubbish on the lawns, I took note of the faces of the people. There were the regulars, long term street people for whom the hospital lawns were their only home. There were bush people, come in from communities and using the lawns as a free open-air hotel. And then there were the blow-ins, mostly white people who'd just arrived in town, scabby-looking desperados for the most part, the lost people of Australia who'd gravitated to Alice Springs the way sewage flows towards a drain hole. It was a fair bet most of these people had warrants out on them back in whatever state they'd come from. They'd chosen the NT because it was as far away as you could get without a passport and they hoped like fuck they couldn't be found up here.

I watched as I worked. One bloke, mid-twenties, had a mohawk that became a dreadlocked mullet at the back. He was wearing a Bintang singlet that looked like it had never been washed and had a scabby looking spiderweb tattoo covering his right shoulder. Was he a junkie desperately trying to escape the smack scene of Melbourne, who'd landed in Alice Springs in a last ditch, do or die, attempt to get away from the smack and get his life back in order? Or was he a long-term jailbird with a record as long as your arm who was dodging the cops down south? Would he make a go of life up here in the NT or had he brought himself with himself, doomed to be a John Doe corpse in the Todd River one day soon?

Someone else caught my eye.

She was sitting alone under an old jacaranda tree in a corner of the hospital lawns. She had a sports bag and a backpack on the grass beside her. She was probably fresh off the bus and they were all her worldly possessions. She had a book open and as I watched she would read a page and a bit, then pause and look around her as if to reassure herself that things were okay, then return to her reading.

She wore a green paisley dress that would have been fashionable in San Francisco in about 1969 but looked slightly too much here and now. She wore a bandana, yellow with some sort of Asian language written in black on it, covering her head which appeared to be completely bald. Maybe she was a cancer patient undergoing chemotherapy.

She was a little different from the usual blow-ins who ended up on the hospital lawns. I worked my way around to where she was, picking up rubbish as I went to make it look legit.

I noticed the Greyhound tags still on her bags when I drew close. They said Darwin, which meant she'd come from the north not the south so perhaps she wasn't a shitbag on the run like the rest of them. I took in the cover of her book, it was *Lord Jim* by Joseph Conrad, a tatty, well-travelled copy. She looked up as I passed by and noticed me watching her. I smiled and said 'Hi.' She warily said 'Hi' back but gave no smile. My offsider and I left to continue our run; I had no idea if I would ever see her again.

About a week later it was my day off and me and my eighteen-month-old daughter were walking to the post office. I checked my box but there was nothing so I turned around to take my little girl for an ice cream.

She was sat on the benches out the front of the post office. She was still wearing the same clothes and was watching the world go by with a vaguely hostile look on her face, as if the ordinary lives of the ordinary people passing by made her feel threatened.

She caught the eye of my daughter who, in her cute toddler way, waved and smiled at her. I watched her face as she processed this unexpected display of goodwill. It took a moment but she slowly, as if out of practice, smiled back at my daughter, real human warmth slowly cracking through.

She timidly waved back at my daughter who smiled and giggled, happy to have made a friend on her outing into town with Dad. We walked on slowly, heading to Uncle Edy's for ice cream but not in any great rush. I looked back over my shoulder and saw her watching us. There was the tiniest trace of a tear in the corner of her right eye. But I could have been mistaken, maybe it was a trick of the light.

I saw her from a distance once or twice after that but never learnt her name or spoke to her. I saw her outside the YHA backpacker joint so I assumed that was where she was staying. I saw her on the bench outside the post office again and once down Todd Mall.

About a month later the NT Police posted her picture on their Facebook page. Concern for welfare it said. Apparently her name was Megan Judd, she was from Bunbury in WA and had been travelling around the country for some time staying in backpacker places, hitching rides, catching the Greyhound bus and generally drifting around. She had last contacted her family from the public phone at a backpacker place in Broome six months ago. She had travelled to Darwin and stayed there for several months before coming to Alice Springs.

The NT Police wanted information from anyone who'd seen her around town.

I decided it was my civic duty to tell the police what little I knew so I rang the number they provided and told my story. The person on the phone wanted to know if I'd seen her with anyone. No, I hadn't, I said, she was always alone when I saw her. Had I ever spoken to her about where she was going? No, I had to admit, I'd never actually said a word to her nor had she said anything to me.

Thanks for your help, the person on the other end of the line said; NT Police might be in touch if they needed further information from me.

For a few days afterwards I kept an eye out hoping I might spot her around town again. Every time I went to the post office I checked the benches out front for her, hoping she might be there, but there was no sight of her. More people came and went from the hospital lawns. No more was heard of her.

REMEMBERING THE DEAD: JUSTIN MORIARTY

I was a lost young man when I met Justin. I had made a hash of my early adult life. At the ripe old age of 20 I'd failed at everything I'd attempted, from starting a band to an abortive attempt at a chef's apprenticeship and a brief stint at being the worst Kirby vacuum cleaner salesman in history. All of it had ended in rejection and humiliation and I was becoming painfully aware that I wasn't winning in life. I'd developed a short but nasty drug habit that had fried my brains and made life even more a struggle than it already was.

In desperation I'd latched onto what I believed was the life saver and safe haven of the Narcotics Anonymous fellowship. I devoured the lingo and belief system of the 12-step movement with the fervent intensity of a religious convert.

Early 2001 saw me living in a place called Ocean View Lodge, and I still remember the address by heart: 100 Hampton Road Fremantle WA 6160. Don't ask me why I still have that rolling around my head, I just do. I was on the dole. It was easier to live in the dole back then, they hassled you less and the money seemed to go further. My life consisted of going to NA meetings, walking around Fremantle and Perth in a daydream and being alone in my room with books and music.

It wasn't much of a life but compared to the drug-ravaged mess my life had been only a year or so previously, it was a huge improvement.

When I call to mind this time, certain impressions return the strongest. The howling wind outside the window of my little room as I read books all afternoon; the bustling streets of Fremantle which I wandered without a goal for hours, those same streets almost deserted at night; the train stations between Fremantle and Perth, the small rooms in the backs of churches where the NA meetings where held.

Mostly what strikes me now as I look back is the sense of time, like that part of my life went on for decades, although in reality it was close to three years maybe. I find it strange how often I do think back to that time now. Here I am a 41-year-old man with a wife and daughter and a fairly good life, fondly reminiscing about living in a doss house on the dole. I once saw an interview with the writer Irvine Welsh, of *Trainspotting* fame, where he said he'd give almost anything to be back in his 20s living in a boarding house doing drugs rather than the successful writer and fifty-year-old man he is now. I think a lot of men feel that way quietly. Youth, even poverty stricken and drug-raddled youth, is better than middle age any day.

Justin started attending the NA meetings around the middle of 2001 and that was where we met. He was living in another, slightly better, boarding house in Fremantle called The Terminus. It was on Pakenham Street and was an old pub that had closed down years ago and been turned into a doss house for losers like us.

Justin fancied himself an intellectual. He told everyone who would listen that he was a writer although as far as I know he never had anything published. Nowadays he would be called a hipster but that term hadn't been invented at the time and he was a lot broker and derelict than the hipsters you see in the inner city these days.

He used to carry whatever novel he was currently reading with him everywhere and make sure people could see the cover. He favoured pretentious über-intellectual European stuff, like Camus, Sartre and some of the Russians, mocking my Anglophile taste for Thomas Hardy and despising my enthusiasm for Australian Literature. I remember him one day sitting at a café on the strip in Fremantle, telling me he had to go home and write. I innocently asked him what he was writing about to which he replied, 'If I could explain it to you I wouldn't have to write it.'

Justin was skinny, partly naturally but also partly from years of drug and alcohol abuse and poor diet. He had a big honker of a nose and I thought initially that he was Jewish but apparently his family was Irish Catholic all the way back. I only know what he told me about his family, they were an old Melbourne family, middle class, they valued education very highly and Justin's two failed attempts at University rankled with them.

Justin didn't take the NA meetings and recovery as seriously as I did. Perhaps because he was older than me he felt less desperate than I did. Repeatedly surviving drug abuse makes a person relaxed about it. He relapsed often and put very little effort into getting better. He plodded along on the sidelines whereas I, believing the 12-step program offered me salvation from the mess I'd made of my life, put plenty of effort into it.

He also had the disdain for others you so often see in pseudo-intellectuals of his type. He would slag off the people in the meetings as soon as we left, belittling their struggles and sometimes mocking their earnest and heartfelt shares in the group. He told me once that I was only listening to my sponsor because I needed a father figure.

The only person he looked up to was a fellow named John Harrison. His story was similar to Justin's. He came from Mittagong in NSW. Middle class family who valued education. Just like Justin he fucked it all up. When I knew him he'd just hit 20 years of going in and out of NA, never staying clean for longer than a year or so, moving from one end of Australia to another, reinventing himself as it suited him. He had been involved with some indie films back east and made a big deal of that. John and Justin would talk utter bullshit to each other about films and books that they never ended up making or writing over coffee on the Fremantle strip.

It was John Harrison who got me seriously thinking about what I was doing with my life. After one of his relapses we spent several hours talking in his little flat in East Fremantle. He was honest for a change, I think he'd had a close call with death on this most recent relapse and it had scared him a little. He started telling me about his life. He told me about growing up in Mittagong, how his older brother was gay and had died from AIDS, how it had fallen to him to go through his brother's possessions and he'd found amyl and heroin stashed away amongst them, how he'd gone in and out of recovery for twenty years with nothing to show for it other than knowing a lot of losers around the country, how he could never go back to the Eastern states because he'd burnt bridges over there.

All of this made a big impression on me at the time. The thought of twenty wasted years, going in and out of NA and drifting around the country really horrified me. I began to want more out of life than the dole and a room in a boarding house.

Justin and I parted company for good in 2003. I flew out of Perth to Brisbane one afternoon. As I waited outside my boarding house for the taxi to the airport Justin came along three quarters pissed. I snapped a few photos of him with a disposable camera I had with me at the time. I still have these photos today. They remind me of the life I used to live and how close I came to going under.

I left Perth and after a few false starts in various places I made a life for myself in Adelaide and was happy for many years. I broke out of that rut I had been in and managed not to go back to it except in my memories, never silly enough to actually physically return there.

In 2008 I was told Justin had gone back to Melbourne and was using heroin again. I bumped into someone I knew from those days on the street when I went for a short holiday to Perth in 2011. He said the last he heard was, several years previously, Justin had been clean and going to meetings in Melbourne for about six months.

Then one day, around Christmas in 2018 I wondered if I could find Justin online. I did a bit of a google search and found his grave on a family history website. Apparently he'd died in 2010, aged 37 years. No wife, no children, no published work, nothing at all to show for his life. Just another one of the lost people of Australia, drifting around this country, sponging off the dole or doing shit kicker jobs. They eventually die and are completely forgotten.

I think about a lot of the people I knew from that time. I would be very interested to know whatever became of John Harrison amongst others. But these people are very hard to find. They leave little or no trace as they wander through life.

REMEMBERING THE DEAD: MATTHEW FITZGERALD

I met Matthew Fitzgerald in January of 2001. It was only a couple of days after New Year's Day, at an NA meeting in the old Pier Street Salvation Army Hall in Perth. I had had an awful Christmas and New Year's. It was my first silly season in recovery and I wasn't enjoying the experience.

After the meeting we sat outside and smoked. Back then a lot more people smoked and the price was still reasonable so you could afford to smoke on the dole. I used to smoke rollies, a lot of people did in recovery, they were cheaper than tailor-made cigarettes. My brand at the time was Samson. The packet had a picture of a roaring lion on it. As I sat near Matthew that day and rolled my smoke while he rolled his, he commented on it.

'Have you had your hair cut by the Philistines?' he asked with a smile. Having grown up in a Christian fundamentalist household I understood the reference and smiled back.

'No, I'm still looking for my Delilah.'

He laughed a little and introduced himself. We sat and chatted for a while. I warmed to him, he seemed very relaxed and happy with life.

He looked like a burnt-out hippy. Like one of those people who really enjoyed the sixties and seventies too much and now have fried brains and keep telling you stories about when they were a roadie for Pink Floyd.

He always wore an Akubra hat which had been battered by time and weather. His hair was long enough to tie into a ponytail and scraggly and unkempt. He had a bung leg and walked with the aid of a stick. He smoked White Ox tobacco which he rolled in liquorice flavoured rolling papers.

We kept meeting each other at meetings over the next few weeks and before long we started having coffee together afterwards. If the meeting was in Perth we'd go to the Old Shanghai Food Hall on James Street in Northbridge. If the meeting was in Fremantle we'd go to Gino's on the strip. We'd only ever have a flat white each, both of us were on welfare and as poor as church mice, but we'd make them last and spend hours chatting.

I have to give credit here and say that Matthew was the first person who told me that I had a talent for stories and should write. We used to both tell yarns. Coffee and cigarettes are excellent fuel for the telling of stories. He told me of his life and I told him of mine. My life up to that point had comprised of growing up in utter misery, raised by Christian fundamentalist parents with a warped view of life and the world, then a few years of drug and alcohol abuse before latching onto 12-step programs like they were a life raft in a stormy sea.

I felt that I hadn't had much of a life yet. That my first run out of the starter's gate had been hobbled and cancelled before I could even really get underway and now here I was, on the dole, going to NA meetings, living in a boarding house with other losers.

But when I told my tales to Matthew, he was engaged by them. He laughed at the funny bits, grew sad at the sad bits, was shocked at the shocking bits. He hung on my words. He was my first audience.

'You have to write this down,' he'd say. 'These are too good to be just between us over coffee, the world needs to hear this.'

I was flattered and began to wonder if he might be right but my self-esteem was pretty low at the time and I didn't feel confident enough to do anything about it. Writers went to universities and had degrees, writers travelled Europe and came back all cultured and shit. I didn't even have a passport, I'd never left Australia and I'd never finished Year 12. Being a writer didn't seem possible to me at the time.

Matthew invited me to his boarding house in Bennett Street, East Perth. The place is now demolished. The mining boom made it too valuable a piece of land to just let it sit and house poor men in squalor. Much more profit to be made in knocking it down and building soulless apartments for the Chinese. When Matthew lived there he showed me a small shed out the back which was actually an old stable. He said it dated from the 1880s when the place was a bakery and the horses used to pull carts that delivered bread all over town. He claimed the owners were doing everything they could to keep it from getting found out by the heritage listing people because they wanted to demolish the place and make big money from it.

I look back on the times I spent with him and they seem happy although I was completely angst ridden and worried about the future. I remember the train back and forth between

Fremantle and Perth. I remember the winter cold as we sat outside the Baptist Church in Northbridge waiting for an NA meeting. I remember the sunshine blessing us like we were God's special children as we sat in the Hay Street Mall and listened to a busker. I remember walking back to the Fremantle Train Station after spending hours at a café talking about life, the universe and everything, the night alive with possibilities.

It is strange that this time of my life, when I had little or no money and barely managed to pay rent on a room in a doss house, seems so significant and meaningful. Whereas later years, when I had savings in the bank and respectable jobs, seem tedious, dismal and pointless.

Matthew told me of his life growing up in the fifties and sixties in Armidale in New South Wales. He told me of his dull and narrow-minded parents and the people in the town. Like every recovering addict I ever met he vividly remembered his first encounter with a mind-altering substance. In his case a bottle of cheap white wine at the age of fifteen. It lit him up in a way nothing else ever had and set him on the road to ruin as he chased that high again and again.

Eventually he left his dull little town and headed to the bright lights of Sydney, just as they were entering the excitement of the Whitlam era. He got in plenty of trouble, ran away to England briefly, burnt bridges and ruined his health at an alarming rate before heading back to Armidale in the hope it would settle him down. It didn't. He described his life during the period between 1979 and 1994 to me as "home, hospital and the pub" and looking into his eyes when he said this I saw the lingering pain of years wasted and life pissed away.

In 1994 he went to his first 12-step meeting and began the journey of recovery. Being free of his addictions he decided to travel a little and see what he could of Australia. His health was still not great but he travelled light and stayed in doss houses in several cities across the country before arriving in Perth and falling in love with the place.

He found a measure of peace and happiness in his life despite owning nothing more than a few clothes and books and living from fortnight to fortnight on the pension.

To discover that this was possible was significant to me. I'd had the Great Australian Dream pushed on me at school and home. Get a steady job, save and buy a house, pay off your mortgage, get a nice car, save for your retirement. It had all been drilled into me from a young age and without realizing I had absorbed this standard. By these standards I was a failure and so was Matthew. The difference was Matthew didn't give a shit and wasn't unhappy about his situation. He did not acknowledge the standard and he was happier for it.

Our friendship grew. We both loved books and turned each other on to our favourites. Matthew introduced me to D. H. Lawrence and Virginia Woolf while I showed him Tim Winton and Irvine Welsh. We were both movie lovers and used to hit the cinema on tight arse Tuesdays. I remember seeing "The Magdalene Sisters" at the old Palace Cinemas in Northbridge, Matthew was deeply affected by it, a legacy of his Catholic upbringing.

Friendship, true friendship, inevitably involves being there for each other when life is a bit shit. I was there when Matthew's mother died. He received the news via one of his sisters who sent him a letter (neither of us owned phones at this time). He rang back using a public phone near the Town Hall in Fremantle and got the details. His mother had died after her second heart attack, the funeral had already happened by the time he got the news, there was nothing for him to do, his presence was not required by his family back east.

He learnt all of this in a ten-minute phone call. Afterwards he re-joined me at an outside table of the little bakery/coffee shop that used to be in the High Street Mall in Fremantle. He told me what had happened and for lack of a better idea I suggested I should grab us both a coffee. He agreed and I got up and went into the shop to get it sorted. When I got back bearing coffee he had moisture around his eyes, hurriedly smeared, as if he had tried to stifle his tears before I got back. I said nothing about it. I was only 21 and these sorts of feelings were a bit beyond my experience.

We drank our coffee slowly and he told me a bit about his mother. How she'd been crushed under his father's domineering nature. How she had once been a beautiful young woman with life ahead of her, full of hopes and dreams, how she had become a baby-making and rearing machine ground down by domestic drudgery and the low expectations of small town life. He told me how his father was the most negative, miserable being he'd ever had the misfortune to meet. How his father had spent most of his existence complaining about his kids, his job and his life, how this had worn down his mother until she was barely a shell of the vibrant young girl she had once been.

Matthew told me, his voice choking up, how he had vowed as a young man to escape and find something more in life than the grim domesticity of his parent's lives. He told me how this vow had sustained him throughout the many misadventures and struggles of his life. When he was strung out and destitute on the streets of Sydney or hospitalised again after a drinking binge, he would tell himself that at least he wasn't married, working at a job he hated to feed kids he didn't really like in a town that suffocated his soul.

He looked around at the people sitting at café tables in the Fremantle sunshine, at the busker down the street, at the pretty girls walking past and the whole scene of vibrant life and he smiled at me. 'Life is pretty good really, let's just be grateful for our blessings.'

I will remember that moment until I die.

A few weeks later his sister sent him some photos of his mother. He showed them to me one day, they were mostly the usual mother and child sort of thing that every family takes but there was one Matthew paused at. His mother just before she married his father. She was only young, nineteen Matthew said, her hair was a mouse brown colour and her face was aglow with life and joy. She looked a beautiful young woman. Matthew looked at it for a long time and then shuffled through the collection until he found another photo. It was his mother again, standing next to his father on their 30th wedding anniversary. She looked tired and worn out, like she needed to sleep for a decade, all the joy and life was gone from her face and a blank, drone expression had replaced it. Matthew and I looked at and compared the two pictures for a long time in silence. A lesson was learned that day.

Around the start of 2003 I began to feel the need to do something more with my life. I was beginning to realise that this idle life I was living couldn't go on forever. I felt I had to get off the dole and get some kind of a job. I still wasn't keen on the whole Great Australian Dream but I wanted more than what I had.

I had also fallen out of love with the whole 12-step recovery thing. I didn't believe in it anymore and began to dislike the losers I met in the meetings. I was tired of hearing dropkicks talk about their feelings and rationalise away their fucked up lives all in the name of recovery.

Everyone I knew in Perth was either in recovery or out using drugs. I didn't see how I could construct a new life for myself in that city. So the obvious solution was to leave and try my luck somewhere else. I began to plan it out.

When I told Matthew what I was thinking he understood but I could tell he was disappointed. I felt like I was betraying our friendship but I didn't let it stop me. I wanted more out of life and this was the only way I could see of getting it. I was convinced there was something better waiting out there for me and nothing was going to stop me getting it.

After a few false starts and failed attempts I managed to get to Adelaide and carve out something of a life for myself. I had more money, was having more sex, lived a bit better and felt like I was part of the great stream of life for the first time ever. I worked as a bouncer around the pubs and clubs of Adelaide and loved it. I got to know all sorts of dubious characters around town; I discovered that women will sleep with you just because you're the man on the door and have a fit body and a confident presence. I took out my father issues on any young idiot who caused trouble in my club; it was fucking great. I felt alive.

All this time I kept in touch with Matthew via good old snail mail. We were faithful letter writers and generally I received and sent a letter every fortnight. I used to love the whole ritual of letter writing, I'd get out my pad and pen, get a coffee and maybe some chocolate and stretch out on the couch in the afternoon and write away. I used to tell Matthew about my adventures as a bouncer and he loved those stories so much. Always he'd insist that I had talent and should become a writer.

After a few years the initial pleasure I had in my new life began to sour. Work became a drag and I felt a little trapped. Bills became harder to pay on a bouncer's wage. Dickheads would try and sue or prosecute you if you bashed them. I began to think I had hit a dead end in life again. I managed to take a trip to Perth and see Matthew in 2006 and it was good to see him again. Perth was in the grip of the mining boom and the old, grotty and seedy city that I had known was reinventing itself as a dynamic, wealthy metropolis. I hated it.

In early 2008 Matthew wrote a letter telling me he was sick, terminally sick, he had bowel cancer and he had a couple months to live at best.

I was horrified. I still carried a sense of guilt for having left him in Perth to seek my own fortune. Now he was dying and I couldn't be there. My wages just wouldn't stretch to a plane ticket and accommodation in Perth.

Over the next few months we wrote to each other every week. Matthew kept me updated with his illness. He got a carer and moved into a hospice. He told me in those final letters that he was okay with dying, it didn't scare him, he was glad he'd had more good than bad in his life and he regretted nothing. He said that he viewed his life as a grand adventure he had shared with some good friends; it was over now but that was no reason to be sad. Nothing lasts forever and he was grateful for the times and friends he'd had.

I wrote back and in one of my most honest moments I asked his forgiveness for leaving. I explained that I had wanted more out of life than the dole, a room in a doss house and NA meetings. I had wanted to live and experience a bit more of life. I never wanted to hurt him or leave him alone but I had to do what I had to do.

He wrote back and said I was silly to worry. He understood that a young man has to make his way in the world and see what he can make of life. He never for a moment bore me any grudge for leaving and he wished me well in all my journeys. He said that he valued our friendship and was glad to have had the times we had together.

Shortly after this he died. I got a letter from his carer explaining the circumstances. According to his wishes he had been cremated and his ashes scattered off the beach in Fremantle. His carer sent me back a large manila envelope containing every letter I'd ever sent to Matthew. Apparently he'd instructed them to be returned to me after his death. I have them still, along with every letter he wrote to me, all in a shoebox together.

REMEMBERING THE DEAD: TERESA

Teresa started going to the NA meetings around Perth about the same time I did, late 2000 and early 2001. She was in the Cyrenian House Rehab for a little while before finding a share house with some other people in recovery. We both used to attend the lunch time meeting held in the little hall out the back of St Alban's Anglican Church in Highgate.

I remember her being very quiet, almost too quiet, with auburn hair and a mousy demeanour. She was quite short as well and faded into the walls of any room she was in. Her voice was barely above a mumble and she never raised it in all the time I knew her.

She had a kind soul once you got past her shyness, and her smile, although it was rare, was a heart-warming thing.

We used to talk before and after the meetings. She was always caring about people in NA, she'd ask after this or that person who had left rehab or hadn't been going to meetings for a while. She seemed to take their failures and relapses to heart. She was very empathic. I think perhaps this contributed to her end. She simply felt too much. Very early on in my time in NA I realised that most people who were currently clean would start using again and most of them would die in active addiction. The numbers just didn't work in your favour. Every month dozens of people got clean, went to rehab, started going to meetings, six months later they were nearly all gone. A very small portion of the annual NA intake made it to one year clean. An even smaller portion made it to two years clean.

I had already developed a certain hardness of heart that made it easier to survive the traumas of my life so this was not an intolerable truth to me. Life was hard, the weak and the stupid get crushed, deal with it, was my attitude. Teresa couldn't or wouldn't harden her heart like this. Every friend of ours in the meetings who wandered off and relapsed hurt her emotionally.

I remember her one day as we sat outside the little hall at St Alban's after a meeting, talking. She was a little upset because a girl named Karen had relapsed again. She wanted to help her. I was of the opinion that Karen had her own path to follow and we couldn't do much about it. In the end I agreed to go with her and see Karen.

Perth before the mining boom was a rundown, broke arse city. There were old houses and flats around the place that hadn't been touched since the Second World War and could be rented out for a song. It was possible in those days to be on the dole and rent out a house and have a low-level drug habit. Nowadays you'd struggle to rent a cupboard on the dole and even a full-time job might not be enough for a basic flat.

Karen was living in this old dump of a red brick house in East Perth that time and developers had forgotten. I remembered the address when I was writing this and tried looking it up on Google street view. Alas, developers have wiped all trace of it and an abomination of glass and steel occupies the site now.

We walked around there in the afternoon and found Karen at home, stoned on heroin. I remember the place was dark, even in the middle of summer. The threadbare carpet barely covered the creaky floorboards and the walls seemed to loom in at us. I've seen some scary shit in my life but that house where Karen lived is the closest I've been to feeling that something was Satanic or possessed. There was an evil vibe there, grabbing at your soul.

Karen acknowledged our presence but was deep into her nod. She wasn't up for an intelligent conversation and Teresa's heartfelt appeals for her to come back to the meetings and have another go at recovery had no effect. There was some other girl there, heavily stoned as well. She was propped up in a corner and in between nods would glare at us like we were there to spoil her fun and ruin her day.

We gave up and went on our way. Teresa had a little cry, as was her habit, and said that she felt terrible that we weren't able to help our friend. I placated her as best I could, telling her that we'd done all we could to help and maybe Karen would come to her senses soon.

Karen ended up coming back to NA for a while and staying clean for a year or so before diving headfirst into a Meth addiction. While under the influence of Meth she ran full speed through a glass sliding door and basically disembowelled herself. Her flat mate at the time, a friend of mine named Adam, called triple zero for the ambulance but Karen bled out before they could arrive. That was the end of Karen, once a promising

Biology student at UWA, dying on the grotty carpet in a cheap flat in Maylands, lying amongst the shattered glass and her own intestines.

Teresa met her own end in early 2002. It was her heart, her inability to not feel everything that happened to and around her, that was probably the root cause of her death.

But that doesn't exonerate Travis.

Relationships are tricky business amongst recovering addicts. The very fact you're in an NA meeting basically proves you're a fuck up. So the obvious question is why the fuck would anyone decent want you? Well, they wouldn't, is the harsh but true answer. The only people who would want you are other fuck ups. Damaged goods attract other damaged goods. Sometimes the various types of dysfunction will click together and more or less work and everyone lives happily, sort of, ever after. More often though the whole thing is toxic and borderline abusive and everyone involved ends up in tears.

Travis had been clean for a year or two. He was a cocky arsehole and I never liked him. Some people just manage to go through life thinking they are the shit and by sheer force of will they convince enough people to agree with them. Travis was one of those people. Now I think being a "cool guy" in NA meetings is a rather pathetic achievement but Travis put a lot of effort into it and quite a few people bought into it.

Sad to say Teresa bought into it, too. She listened to him talk utter horse shit in meetings with a doe-eyed expression on her face. Travis had the classic predator's instinct and saw vulnerable female flesh. It was a disaster.

They were only a couple for a month or two but that was all that was needed to throw Teresa's already fragile state of mind for six. She simply couldn't cope with the stress of a relationship at that point in her life. That would have been true even if it was a normal, vaguely healthy relationship but the toxic power plays and bullshit Travis put her through were just too much.

Within two months she was using again. I didn't see her for a while. I heard rumours from people, none of them good, she'd been seen at various known heroin hotspots around Perth. Nobody could reach her.

I felt sad but I had already got into the habit of hardening my heart to this sort of thing. I had accepted that people were going to do what they were going to do and there was very little I could do about it.

I saw her for the last time, I think it was early March of 2002, at a bus stop on Beaufort Street just up from the Brisbane Hotel. I was on my way to the lunch time meeting at St Alban's and I saw her there waiting for the bus into the city. I could tell she was using heroin again right away. She had her face hidden with sunglasses and was shivering despite the temperature being in the low 30s.

For a moment I wanted to stop and say something. I thought about asking her if she was alright, if she wanted to come to the meeting with me, if there was something I could do to help. But I didn't. I kept walking and said nothing. I know she saw me. I don't know if it would have helped if I'd stopped. It is one of my few deep regrets that I didn't stop and say something to her that day.

A few weeks later she was dead.

The news filtered through the NA meetings the way it always did. Some people were really upset, others not so much, some people took the news as a spur to continue with their recovery, others seemed to use it as an excuse to start using heroin again.

Travis, the despicable piece of shit who was at least partly the cause of her death, used the news to talk about himself. He shared in meetings about how he felt like his recovery had been set back to day one because of the whole experience. He made it sound like he was the real victim here.

I had never heard such blatantly selfish bullshit spoken in public before. I was shocked and expected to see other people as angry about it as I was. But instead people were lapping it up. I learnt a valuable lesson that day; a little charisma and some slick words can make a sociopath not only acceptable in society but actually admired. I looked around the room and saw other women looking at Travis with that same doe-eyed admiration Teresa had. It sickened me.

It was about this time that I started to fall out of love with the whole NA thing. I realized most of the people in the meetings weren't going to be saved and even if they were most of them weren't worth saving. It was effectively a day care for losers and if I wanted more out of life I had to move on from it.

I did end up leaving it all behind a year or so later. I made a life for myself in another city and did the best I could at the time. I never forgot Teresa and I never stopped wishing I had stopped and talked to her that day on Beaufort Street. She was a good, sweet person and despite her faults she didn't deserve to die the way she did and at such a young age, too.

DROWN THE OLEANDER

She had been sniffling for a day or two but didn't really get sick until the Friday afternoon. Russell arrived home from work and his wife, Sharon, had their daughter Elizabeth wrapped up in bed already, even though it was still light outside.

'She's burning up, it's been getting worse all day.'

Russell placed his hand on his little girl's forehead. 'She's cooking alright, what are we going to do?'

'Just the usual, bed rest, keep her warm and give her lots of fluids. I've got to work tomorrow so you're looking after her.'

Russell nodded. It looked like being a miserable wet weekend anyway so staying home with a sick child wasn't really a burden. He'd watch the footy and keep an eye on her at the same time.

Saturday morning arrived and Sharon dressed in her scrubs and headed to the Hospital for her shift. Russell checked in on Elizabeth when he got up. She was awake but didn't look well, the fever still burning her up and her pyjamas drenched in sweat.

'Alright, Lizzy?'

She nodded faintly in response.

'How about you have a shower and get some new PJs on and I'll make us some breakfast?'

'Ok, Dad'

She trudged slowly towards the bathroom, her hair soaked in sweat and ratty as it limped down her shoulders. Russell felt sorry for his little girl but if she was well enough to walk to the bathroom unaided she wasn't actually dying. He made himself a cup of coffee while she showered.

Elizabeth took much longer than normal to shower. If she had been well and if her mum had been home she'd have been yelled at to hurry up and stop using all the hot water but Russell was happy to let her procrastinate for now.

He sipped his coffee and looked out the kitchen window. The rain had really set it. Fucking Adelaide winters, he thought, I wish I lived somewhere warm. Elizabeth eventually finished her shower and dressed in her room. She left her hair wet as if drying it was too much bother and sidled up to Russell and leaned against him.

'You dying, are you, Lizzy?'

'I feel horrible, Dad.'

'Well, we'll get some breakfast into you and you can sleep it off. How's that for a plan?'

'I'm not hungry, Dad.'

'You've got to eat sweetheart, the body needs fuel to fight the germs. How about some toast? Vegemite?'

Elizabeth nodded reluctantly and flaked out on the couch.

Russell got busy in the kitchen as the rain drummed hard on the roof, drowning out every other sound.

He brought her a plate of Vegemite toast and a glass of apple juice.

'Get this into you, Lizzy.'

He watched her eat. Her bites were pensive, unsure, as if Vegemite toast was a struggle for her fever-wracked body. Her frailness triggered some tender fatherly emotion beyond what he normally felt. He would have died for her in that instant if it could have made her well again. He reached out his hand and stroked her hair gently.

She finished her toast, or as much of it as she was ever going to eat, and at his insistence she drank all the juice down. She said she wanted to sleep again so he got her a blanket and pillow from the cupboard in the hall and they curled up on the couch. Like a kitten finding a warm spot she was asleep in minutes. Russell touched her forehead and felt the heat radiating off her body. The fever was still strong.

He pondered what to do while she was asleep. He didn't want to bang around in the kitchen making breakfast in case the noise woke her up. He would make Vegemite toast.

He needn't have worried about making enough noise to wake her up. The rain at that very moment kicked up another notch and grew louder and more intense than it had been all morning. He looked out the screen door into the backyard. Sodden, absolutely soaked. Put your foot down in that and you'll be ankle deep in mud.

He sat back down with his toast and coffee on the couch next to his sleeping daughter. He ate, it rained some more, Elizabeth stirred a little in her sleep, he put his hand on her forehead again and checked her temperature, the morning passed by. Inside the house was silent while outside the rain thumped down.

He looked at the time and wondered if there might be footy on TV yet. Cautiously he turned it on and quickly turned the sound down so as not to wake her. He flicked through the channels until he found a game about to start. St Kilda vs Carlton, they were still doing all the pre-game nonsense so he settled in to watch it with the sound turned down low.

Elizabeth woke up halfway through the second quarter, startled, not sure why she was waking up in the lounge room instead of her own bedroom. She looked around, puzzled and unsure. Russell put a soothing hand on her shoulder.

'You feeling any better, sweetheart?'

'Really thirsty.'

'I'll get you another juice then.'

She sat up as he went to the kitchen. Her tired, feverish eyes tried to focus on the football. Instead, her ears caught the sound of rain outside.

'How long's it been raining, Dad?'

'All day, doesn't look like stopping either.' Russell said, handing her a glass of juice.

She sipped her juice and closed her eyes in a tired, fuzzy way.

'Tell me a story, Dad.'

Russell watched her.

'You're getting a bit old for bedtime stories, aren't you?'

'Not a bedtime story for kids. Tell me a story, about your life or something.'

Her voice was a little hoarse from the fever and dehydration, so it sounded like a plea. He didn't really have the heart to refuse her and the game wasn't that interesting anyway.

'Well, let me think. I don't know what to tell you, sweetie.'

'Tell me about when you and Mum met.'

He smiled. He knew he'd told her this one before, but it was a good story though and it had a happy ending.

'Well, I was up in Port Hedland, it was, well you're nine now so it must have been thirteen years ago now and I ....'

'How come you were in Port Hedland?'

'I was looking for work, trying to get in the mining game to make some big money. Adelaide was a bit grim for jobs back then. Well, it still is, truth be told, so a lot of young blokes headed to WA because the mines were going gangbusters at the time. So I was there, I didn't end up getting into the mines, I didn't have all the right tickets, see, but I got a job driving a delivery van around the town and that wasn't too bad.'

'Where was Mum?'

'I'm getting to that bit. Anyway, so I was driving a delivery van around town during the week and on the weekends I'd go fishing. The water up there, sweetie! It's warm and clear and full of fish. So anyway, this one day I get a bite and I start reeling it in, it feels heavy and I'm thinking I've got a big snapper or something. Turns out to be a stingray!'

Elizabeth smiled a sleepy, happy smile, full of warmth and love.

'Well, I get it to the surface and it flicks its tail at me and stings me!'

He flicked his forearm to illustrate his saga.

'So, there I am with a puncture wound in my bicep from a stingray barb and the poison starts working and I'm in a world of hurt! So, my mate that I was with at the time takes me to the hospital and guess who the nurse was?'

'Mum?'

'Yep, pretty as a picture. Anyway one thing lead to another after that and here you are, Lizzy.'

'What did they do to stop the stingray poison?'

'Ah, well the treatment for a stingray wound is hot water, as hot as you can stand it, poured directly onto the site of the wound. They basically just boiled up a kettle and poured it on me. Still got the scar.'

Elizabeth leaned onto her father's shoulder; her feverish head stained his shirt with sweat as he stroked her hair again.

'I like that story, Dad. You should tell it more often.'

'I usually do on our anniversary, after I've had a couple drinks, of course.'

He chuckled and gave her a quick hug. She settled back under her blanket on the couch and in a few minutes her steady breathing indicated she was sleeping.

He tried to watch the rest of the game but he'd lost the thread of it and his mind was wandering now. He thought back to those days. The hope he'd had when he left Adelaide for the Pilbara; his grand plans to get a mining job and make big money, invest it all in real estate and live the good life. It hadn't worked out like that. He'd been on the edges of the mining boom; he'd made more money than he would have if he'd stayed in Adelaide but nothing like what he'd hoped.

And of course, he'd ended up back in Adelaide. Nobody escapes this town, he thought, you try and find something better out there but somehow you end up back here. Every so often down the shops or at the servo he bumped into someone from high school. After all these years they were all still here. Still in ruts that were probably carved for them before they were born. Nobody escapes Adelaide.

He sighed. He got up and stood at the back screen door. He looked out on the wet backyard. The rain had slowed down a little, but then, as if to mock him, the sky cracked open and it started pouring down hard again.

He remembered rainy days like this when he was a kid. He'd lived with miserable Adelaide winters all his life except for those couple of years in WA. The need to escape surged up in him. He could do it, he thought, pack them all up and head back to WA, back to the Pilbara, no more Adelaide winters, no more grim, dull life in this grim, dull city.

He felt Shannon's arm slip around him, momentarily startled he looked around and saw her still in her scrubs.

'How'd you go, babe?' she asked.

'All good, she's slept most of the day; still got a fever though.'

She snuggled into him more.

'You feel hungry? I'm thinking I'll jump online and order us some Indian. Fancy a lamb korma? With some naan bread?'

He nodded. She looked out into the backyard through the screen door.

'Everything's soaked out there! It's going to drown my poor oleander!'

Good, he thought to himself, drown everything in this fucking city. Drown it all and wash it away so we can start again somewhere else.

'Mum? Dad?'

He turned to Elizabeth, his heart softening.

'It's alright, Lizzy,' he said, 'we're here.'

THE FOX AND
THE FISHERMAN

My Uncle Daryl was a good old boy. Loved his footy and cricket, loved fishing and camping, loved women but didn't have much luck with them. His type is frowned upon and denigrated in modern Australia but blokes like him were the backbone of this country once.

He used to take me fishing a lot when I was young. I think I was a substitute for the son he never had. As I grew older the fishing trips grew longer, he'd take me camping and fishing for a week, sometimes two; it was great.

One trip I remember well was to a place called Ebor in New South Wales. It's up in the ranges between Armidale and Coffs Harbour. I was fourteen so it must have been 1994; it was the school holidays, tail end of winter, start of spring, still cold but starting to warm up. Daryl had an old Land Rover Defender then, an ex-military one he'd bought at an auction. He'd set it up for fishing trips and you could comfortably live out of the back of it for a couple of weeks.

We went to Nambucca Heads first. My grandparents, Daryl's parents, were living there at the time. We spent a few days with them and I caught a beautiful Rock Cod off the rock wall one afternoon. We drove to Ebor at first light one morning, the diesel engine spluttering its way up the mountains through Dorrigo.

I remember we had dinner the first night at the pub there in Ebor. It was a grand old building, I hope it's still standing, one of those old country pubs that were built at the arse end of the Victorian era when things were built to last. Solid red brick and cornices, walking upstairs to the rooms was like stepping back in time, you half expected to hear news of the siege of Mafeking, the immersion in the past was that strong. I loved it. Even now when I'm travelling around the country I try and find these sorts of places.

We sat at the bar and had schnitzel, chips and gravy for dinner. Daryl struck up a conversation with the local blokes and soon they were happily chatting away about fishing, footy and cricket, old-fashioned masculinity in action. I remember one of the local blokes had his daughter with him, she was about the same age as me. I remember her hazel eyes and cattle-dog brown hair. I was too awkward and shy to go over and talk to her though. I really was an awkward teenager.

The next morning we headed out to the fishing spot Daryl had found last time he'd been there. The area around Ebor is very hilly and full of little creeks and streams; half of them don't have names and are barely visited by anyone. Someone at some point introduced trout to these waters and they have thrived ever since. Daryl's plan was to teach me to fly-fish for trout.

We stopped near one of the streams and started getting organized. Daryl had brought me a set of waders to wear that were a little too big. He pulled out the fly-fishing rods and started teaching me the basic technique. Fly-fishing is one of those things that looks a lot easier than it actually is. I struggled a bit.

'All in the wrist, young mate,' Daryl would say, 'just got to give it the right amount of flick at the right time and she's apples.'

I tried and slowly my wrist managed the flick in the correct fashion. Daryl decided I was good enough and we headed to the water.

It was a lot colder than I had thought it would be. The waders kept me dry but not warm.

'Makes yer' balls go up in yer' guts, doesn't it?' Daryl said and he wasn't wrong.

I started making casts the way he'd taught me and getting my fly on the water. I got the hang of it and soon grew used to the cold and started to enjoy myself. I didn't get so much as a nibble all that morning so I spent a lot of time looking around at the scenery. The creek was a mixture of native scrub and feral blackberry bushes. Past this was open pasture country with a few random Herefords grazing. Here and there were clumps of big, old trees, some eucalyptus, some pine, all big and ancient. I remember thinking that some of these trees must have pre-dated white settlement and I was probably right.

As I was looking around and daydreaming, Daryl had worked his way along the riverbank further downstream. His dedication paid off and he bagged two nice trout in the space of ten minutes. He pointed out a dead cow on the side of the river twenty metres further down and credited it for his success.

'All the flies and maggots and what not are in the area for that dead beastie, some of them fall in the water and get eaten by the trout here so the trout hang around and get into feeding mode. Then it's just a matter of me coming along and bagging a winner or two.'

I couldn't argue with his fishing wisdom but I did wonder why the cow had died.

'Who knows? Could have eaten something nasty, could have just been old and had it. Whichever farmer it belongs to will work it out eventually. There's a fox on it just now though, having a free feed like a cheeky bugger.'

I looked and there was indeed a red tail in the air. I couldn't see the fox's head because it was buried in beef as the little scavenger tore off as much rotting meat as the size of its jaws would allow.

'He's getting while the getting's good,' Daryl chuckled to himself, and cast his line back into the stream.

I continued staring at the creature as he gorged himself. Periodically the fox's head would pop up and he'd chew the meat he'd ripped from the carcass.

I had no luck the rest of the morning although Daryl bagged another decent trout. We were pretty cold and wet by midday and decided to have a break. We returned to the Land Rover and Daryl boiled a billy to make hot chocolate for us both. We sat and sipped our brews and watched the scenery in perfect contentment. A family of currawongs flew past noisily but otherwise the country was silent.

While we were sitting around enjoying the serenity a ute drove down the dirt track to our spot. It was one of the local blokes we'd met in the pub the night before and his daughter, the girl I'd noticed but been too shy to talk to.

'This'll be the locals checking up on us, making sure we're not trashing the joint,' Daryl predicted as the vehicle approached.

'How's the fishing going?' the man said as he stopped the ute and leaned out the window.

Daryl waved. 'Couple middle-sized trout but no record breakers yet.' The girl watched us from her side. For a moment she made eye contact with me and I, rather predictably, immediately fell in love with her.

'Got a cow missing, supposed to be on the other side of the river but it might have snuck over here, have you seen it?'

'Well, there's a dead one just downstream about a hundred metres or so. It's on the bank on this side, been there a day or two, I'd say. There was a fox tucking in when we were down there just before.'

The man grimaced.

'I fucking thought so. Well, we'd better check it out, best of luck with your fishing.'

He waved and drove off. As he did the girl turned and looked at me. Her hair, cattle-dog brown and shining in the weak midday sun, fell over her left eye. The ute rounded a bend in the track and disappeared from view.

Daryl had his opinions about the matter.

'Farmers are grim bastards. The whole farming game is either feast or famine and it's mostly luck which one of those you get. That cow is worth money to him, he's calculating right now how much he's lost and how much he can make back from the rest of his livestock. Fucking hard way to go through life, if you ask me.'

I was still thinking about the girl with the cattle-dog brown hair but later on when I'd returned to Earth it occurred to me that Daryl had managed to nestle himself into his job as a council worker and milk the ratepayers for 18 years at that point. He knew a thing or two about avoiding the hardships of life and the perils of the economy.

Daryl made us some lunch, gutted his trout and put them in the esky for dinner. While we were having lunch a shot rang out from the direction of the cattle carcass.

'That'll be the end of old mate foxy,' Daryl said.

We went back to fishing in the afternoon. The water was slightly warmer but still cold enough to make you wince on first contact. I finally caught a respectable trout and Daryl's luck went to shit. We gave up while it was still light, set up the tent and started settling in for the night. Daryl cooked our trout over the fire with potatoes and butter. We ate and talked about nothing much as the sun went down. Our sleeping bags began to call us and we were asleep before long.

I woke up at some point in the night, probably a little after midnight. I needed to piss. I got up without waking Daryl and put my boots on outside the tent. I walked a little distance from our camp because I knew from previous trips that Daryl hated people pissing near the camp. The moon was about three quarters full and I could see quite well. I wandered off a little down towards the water and a tree that I decided would be good enough for a pissing post.

As I walked closer I spotted it. The fox, bullet hole through its shoulder, strung up on a branch with a little rope tied to its tail, dangling in the moonlight like a lynching victim. I'd seen this before; some farmers had a theory that putting them out on display like this would scare off the others. A memento-mori of the crudest, most bumpkin kind.

I stood there in the darkness with my full to bursting bladder wondering about the man who'd done it and his daughter.

COOKING BREAKFAST
FOR HARRIET

The dullest exteriors can hide passions as violent as a cyclone. The people we think of as being as plain as an arrowroot biscuit may have emotional storms that we don't see.

Even places that seem safe and boring usually conceal rages and lusts fit for a true crime book series. Take Adelaide, Australia's dullest capital city, which is reputed to have more serial killers and child rapists per head of population than anywhere else in the country.

On this particular dull Sunday morning in the dull city of Adelaide there was a dull block of flats on the corner of Goodwood Road and Francis Street. They were the sort of dreary place you would drive past and pay no attention to at all. Populated mostly by young working people with a sprinkling of old age pensioners and Indian immigrants, they were pleasant enough to live in but it would take a special eye to call them interesting or beautiful.

In one of those flats a man was waking up next to a woman.

For a split second it startled him to see the woman next to him. He'd been on his own for a while and had grown used to it. Then he remembered who she was and why she was here.

He'd answered her phone call the previous morning.

'I'm coming back,' she'd said.

He'd sighed over the phone at her.

'Are we still doing this shit?' The exasperation in his voice said volumes. She'd grown desperate and pleading.

'No, I really mean it. I made a mistake leaving you, I see that now. This time in Sydney has been a waste. All I want to do is be back with you.'

He was silent. She played her final card.

'Well, my flight arrives at six. If you don't show up, if you don't want me, I suppose I'll find a place in a women's shelter or something.'

Let her stay in a women's shelter, he thought. She left me, she made her bed and she can lie in it. But he was waiting for her when she got off the plane. She slipped her arms around him and held him close and kissed him and it was like she'd never been away.

Now here she was, in his bed, wearing his trackpants and t-shirt because she had been too tired and disorganised to unpack her bags before flaking out for the night. She'd fallen asleep before night had even properly fallen. Why she was so tired he hadn't asked. Then she had awakened about one-ish in the morning, rather insistently had initiated sex with him, then unceremoniously passed out again.

He knew he was being used.

He got up without waking her and pottered around the flat unsure of his next move. He made coffee and found the gift she had brought him from Sydney. For years now he'd rather haphazardly collected souvenir coffee mugs from places he'd visited. In the cupboard now was a dozen or so mugs, one from

Perth with a cartoon Black Swan on it, one from Port Lincoln with a stylised tuna leaping out of the water and now to add to them was the one she'd just brought him. He turned it around in his hand. *Sydney, the harbour city* was written in bold letters on a background showing the Harbour Bridge and the Opera House.

She'd given it to him with a smiling face, as if this was a baby they'd made together, as if this made her two months in Sydney alright. For the briefest second he felt like smashing the mug over her head, caving in her skull with it and laughing as the blood stained the mug and made the picture of the bridge invisible.

He'd smiled and thanked her and put it in front of his other mugs on the shelf.

Now, because he couldn't see the point in not using it, he was spooning coffee into it. A small but significant surrender.

The noise of the kettle and the smell of his coffee woke her up. She sidled up and sat next to him on the couch.

'Morning Babe, oh it's good to be home!' She wrapped her arms around him in an exaggerated hug that threatened to spill his coffee.

Home, he thought, she's calling my place home. He should put his foot down, he thought, put her in her place and remind her that *she* left *him* not the other way around, so she had no right to go getting so comfortable now. But then she's home, he thought, she's back with me and this time she'll stay, we're going to make a home together.

They snuggled together on the couch, her kisses and cuddles destroying whatever resistance he had left.

'I'll make us brekkie' he said.

'Sure,' she replied quietly.

Within a few minutes the flat smelled of bacon, eggs and beans. He felt happy and sang a jaunty tune to himself. He was cooking breakfast for Harriet, his girl. Sure, they'd had two months apart but that was then, this is now. He was looking forward to a good feed and then maybe some nice, unrushed sex in the afternoon.

He heard her bolt off the couch. He heard the toilet seat fly up and the sounds of vomiting. He left the bacon to simmer and stood in the bathroom door. She had her hair pulled back with one hand and with the other hand supported herself bent over the toilet. A little dribble and bile was just trickling from her lips. She turned to look at him.

Morning sickness.

'I'm sorry babe, the cooking smell sets me off. I'm alright most mornings.'

'How far gone are you? Is it mine?'

She closed her eyes and braced herself to answer.

'About two months, I think it's yours, I'm pretty sure it is. That time just before I left. There was one guy in Sydney but I don't think it's his.'

He stood there breathing deep. She spat some remaining bile into the toilet and turned her head to look at him again.

'I'm sorry babe, I didn't mean for this to happen.'

Her voice was almost pitiful, pleading now.

'Get yourself sorted and come and have breakfast,' he said. He very nearly added that she was eating for two now.

He stood in the kitchen watching the bacon slowly sizzle and listening to her wash her face. He picked up the mug she'd given him, looked again at the little picture of the Harbour Bridge and the Opera House. She'd been in that city for two months, he thought, left me with barely a goodbye and went there doing god knows what and fucking god knows who and now she's up the duff and looking to me to play daddy to a kid that might not even be mine.

The dull rage inside him bubbled along like the frying bacon.

Harriet emerged from the bathroom.

'Babe, could I just have some cereal? I don't think I can hold greasy fried bacon down; you know what I mean?'

She caught the expression on his face.

Without realizing it his grip on the coffee mug had grown tighter and tighter. Now, hearing her voice, knowing what she'd done, knowing she had planned to take him for a mug, he threw the cup.

It caught the top of her forehead. The cup ricocheted off her head and smashed into pieces against the wall. Harriet stumbled back, trapped against the kitchen wall.

'OUT!' he roared

'OUT YOU SLUT!'

The bacon blackened in the pan and the neighbours debated calling the police.

FAR FROM YOUR FATHER'S COUNTRY

Daniel had known Naomi exactly four months when they checked out of rehab together.

The place was called Cockatoo Hill. It was hidden away in the northern part of Sydney, just before you hit the big national park and was close enough to the water that they could smell the salt in the air if the wind was blowing right. The place was surrounded by Norfolk Island pines and casuarina trees and in the afternoons cockatoos would descend on the trees and mangle them with their beaks.

Daniel was an oddity at the rehab. Not because he was a heroin addict, there were plenty of those, but because he was a West Australian. The rehab had people from every part of the Eastern States but in his four months there he was the only person from WA.

Perhaps the loneliness and dislocation were too much for him. Perhaps if he'd gone to a rehab in Perth he might have coped better. At any rate, the four months he spent there were an ashen wasteland of crippling depression and loneliness and in hindsight it was inevitable that he would latch on to the first person who showed him some emotional warmth.

Naomi was from Brisbane originally but had spent several years in Sydney where the bulk of her drug use had taken place. She was chatty and flippant about it all. She seemed to know a lot of people in the rehab from various times and places in her dubious past. She would casually explain how she knew the new arrivals to Daniel.

'He used to be a dealer around the Darlinghurst area a few years back. He did a little bit of time in jail, but it didn't slow him down much.'

'She used to go out with this guy I knew back in Brisbane who cooked meth. She got pregnant, but they took the baby off her because she was completely toxic with drugs.'

'She used to share a flat with me when I first came to Sydney. Fuck, we had some mad times back then.'

Listening to all this, Daniel had the impression the east coast of Australia was a loose association of drug-using hipsters divided by two degrees of separation at the very most. He imagined a sort of Freemason's network of people doing drugs while still managing to look cool, stretching from Melbourne to Brisbane.

They fell into what is commonly called a "rehab romance" and against all advice they checked out together four months into a six-month program.

Their first night out of the rehab they stayed in a small room above a pub in the city, not far from Central Station. They had very little money so they ate Macca's for dinner and settled into their room for the night. They hadn't been able to consummate their relationship while in rehab, such things are strictly policed by the counsellors, so they made love for the first time in the grotty room with paint peeling from the roof. It was the first time in over a year that Daniel had had sex, the first time in over five years that he'd had sex not under the influence of drugs or alcohol, and it blew his tiny little mind.

Naomi's body had held up against the ravages of drug use fairly well, a few small scars on her arms and hands but basically still the body of a twenty-five-year-old woman in reasonable health. Daniel was smitten. His common sense, that little voice questioning whether this was such a great idea or not, was drowned out in a tidal wave of lust and loneliness.

They didn't use a condom and Daniel came inside her without a thought to the consequences.

The next day they had breakfast at Macca's and walked to Central Station where they boarded a bus for Brisbane. Naomi had organised for them to live with her parents in the downstairs of their old Queenslander. Daniel spent most of the trip watching the scenery. The East Coast is so different to West Australia, much more built up, barely any gaps between the little towns and so much greenery. His mind strayed back to the family trips from Geraldton to Perth when he was a kid. The flatness and dryness of it all, the big empty spaces between the small towns and most significantly the ocean to the west side of you, not the east.

They arrived at Roma Street Station after dark. Naomi's parents picked them up, they barely acknowledged Daniel and glared at their daughter.

'It was supposed to be a six month program in that Rehab,' Naomi's father said. She made no defence of her actions.

Daniel and Naomi slept in a bed that was so stained and threadbare it looked ready for the tip. Too tired to make love they flaked out straight away without a plan for tomorrow.

Daniel woke up first and the reality of where he was really hit him for the first time. On the wrong side of the country from everyone and everything he'd ever known, shacked up with a woman he'd only met a few months ago, a barely tolerated guest of her parents, still recovering from five years of heroin use and to top it all off, he was unemployed and had been for a long time. He held his head in his hands as a wave of depression followed by terror overwhelmed him. What if Naomi or her parents told him to leave? Where would he go? What would he do?

He calmed himself, told himself that he'd been in and survived worse situations than this many times before. He repeated this simple mantra to himself until he felt ready to face things. He decided that he could at least try and do something about his employment status. He showered, shaved and dressed and found Naomi's parents in the kitchen.

'Hey, could you tell me where the nearest bus stop is? I want to go get started job hunting.'

They seemed somewhat taken aback by his get up and go but were helpful.

'Just go around the corner to the main road, the bus stop this side is for going into the city, the one on the other side of the street takes you out to Chermside.'

He did the rounds all that day and half the next day, dropping resumés and approaching any place where he might possibly have a chance: bottle shops, cafés and servos. In the end a small local servo gave him a trial shift. He felt better about his dubious life choices as he filled out the employment paperwork they gave him. It wasn't much of a job, but it meant he was off the dole and he felt vaguely respectable when they put him on as a casual. Naomi's parents started being a little bit nicer to him, saying good morning and asking how his day went. Life was looking up.

He continued to live with Naomi in the downstairs part of the old Queenslander. He was still smitten with her, they continued to have sex without taking any precautions, as careless and unthinking as wild mice. Naomi showed no inclination to try and find a job, preferring to remain on the dole. She spent her days visiting people she knew from back in the day, catching up with the extended social network she seemed to have. When Daniel came back from work she would fill him in on who she'd met that day and what they'd been up to.

'You remember I told you about my friend, Nicole? Well, she's having another baby, but she broke up with the guy who is the father. She's not sure if she should tell him or not.'

'I met my friend Anna down the street today, oh my god! It's been years since I saw her, she's changed so much, she thought I was still in Sydney, oh and she told me what happened to my ex, you won't believe this but ...'

A gossip column that Daniel didn't understand or care about.

Daniel was the only one of the pair taking recovery seriously, making the effort to attend a couple of NA meetings a week.

'Those meetings are such a downer,' Naomi said. 'I had enough of that shit in rehab. Why go and listen to other people share their dramas?'

Daniel wanted to point out that listening to other people's dramas was basically all she did with her friends, but he didn't.

Daniel made friends at the NA meetings, deliberately avoiding the people who seemed to take recovery casually, seeking out those with serious minds like his own. Tony was older than him, in his early 40s although the ravages of heroin addiction made him look older. From an old Italian family down in Footscray in Melbourne, he had a serious mind and treated recovery like it mattered. Most importantly, he was willing to listen when Daniel needed to talk.

On days when Daniel wasn't working at the servo they would go to a meeting and hit a coffee shop afterwards. The simple pleasures of caffeine and friendship substituting for their former narcotic vices.

Tony talked a lot about time, how much of it he'd wasted, how much of it he had left, what could be made of what he had left.

'You know young fella, I started using when I was 17, got clean when I was 39, that's 22 years flushed down the drain. Add to that a couple of prison stints; you know I've been in prison in three different states? Geelong prison in Victoria, Silverwater in New South Wales and the old Boggo Road here in Queensland. Some fucking achievement, isn't it? Now I'm 42, got three years clean under my belt, still just taking it a day at a time, but the numbers! That's the shit that haunts me. I wake up some nights and think about those numbers, all that time gone, can't get a single day of it back, and then I think about how long I might have left to live. Maybe another thirty years? Forty years? Knowing my luck now that I'm clean, I'll get fucking cancer or something.'

'I remember the first time I put a needle in my arm. I was 17 years old, I remember it like it was yesterday. It was in a squat in Footscray where a bunch of shitbag skater kids hung out, I remember it rained outside and I nodded and watched the rain for hours. 22 years later I checked into a rehab here in Brisbane. All that time just went past like sand through my fingers and here I fucking am.'

'I try not to be bitter. I try to keep focused on the here and now, I think about what I might do with my life now that I'm in recovery. But it's always there, that sense of loss, and then comes the anger. If things had been different my life might have gone down another road. If only I'd done this instead of that, if only, if only. And now here I am, a 42-year-old ex-junkie who works part time and goes to NA meetings during the week. I know it could be worse, I know I should be dead multiple times over, I know that every day clean is a victory but it just doesn't feel that way sometimes.'

Daniel nodded and sipped his coffee. He had lost years of his life to addiction, granted only five compared to Tony's twenty-two, but the loss still ached. The question of what to do with whatever life remained was just as haunting. He knew that working at the servo and living in the downstairs part of Naomi's parent's house was only a temporary thing. He needed a direction, a plan, something.

The rapturous love he had felt with Naomi was fading. Most of all he wanted to go home, to Western Australia, to his family if they would have him back.

'I feel like a fucking alien over here,' he told Tony one day over coffee. 'Like I'm in another country. Everything about the eastern states seems wrong to me. Too many people, everything is crammed together, the ocean is on the wrong side, everyone knows each other and has history together. I feel like a foreigner. I just can't escape this feeling I've taken a drastically wrong turn in my life. Like I was never supposed to be here in this place with this woman. Like that movie, I can't remember what it was called, where the person has like two timelines, one where she catches the train and some things happen and another one where she misses the train and different stuff happens. Well, I think I'm on the wrong timeline, like I wasn't supposed to come over to the eastern states, like I wasn't supposed to meet Naomi.'

'I wonder if there is another timeline where I stayed in WA and different stuff happened? I keep having this dream where I'm a kid again and we are on holiday at Dongara just being beach bums all summer. I'm with my cousins and we're all jumping off the jetty into the water and we're happy and young and free. Then I wake up and I'm in bed with a woman I met in rehab a few months ago, in the house her parents are letting us stay in, in a city I don't know, on the wrong side of the country. I don't know how I got here, this is not the way my life was supposed to go, this is not where I am supposed to be. But I don't know what to do about it.'

Tony sipped his coffee and asked the question on his mind.

'Could you leave Naomi and go back to WA?'

Daniel shrugged and fiddled with his teaspoon as if it helped him think.

'I don't know, I thought I loved her but maybe that was just the loneliness of rehab and the sudden shock of being clean after so many years using. I had no time to get any sort of stability. Like there I was one minute, fucked up on the gear, then all of a sudden I'm on the wrong side of the country, shacked up with a woman I've just met. I had no in-between time to get my bearings.'

'Maybe I could leave her. I've left women before and survived. I have a little bit of money from the servo job, enough for a plane ticket to Perth. It's possible, I suppose.'

Tony put down his coffee cup and breathed in deeply.

'Well, mate, if you go I'll miss our chats but you've got to do what's right for your life. In the end you're the person who has to live it. All I can say is, don't sacrifice your recovery. If you're clean then you can salvage something good out of whatever direction you go in life. If you're using again everything is going to go to shit. Remember, if you're clean you have options, you have hope. If you're using you don't have either.'

'You want more out of life than a dole cheque and a drug habit. Does Naomi?'

Daniel wandered around the city a little more. He walked through the malls and watched the people shopping and eating, normality still strange to him after years on the fringes of society.

The next couple of weeks drifted past without change. He picked up some more shifts at the servo because someone had quit, he continued to go to NA meetings and catch up with Tony. Naomi remained essentially idle, visiting her friends and lounging about at home. Her parents started to like him more and more. Her father in particular talked to him like an equal now, looking him in the eyes, asking how his day was in a casual, friendly way. It was remarkable how the mere act of getting a job made him socially acceptable in their eyes.

The financial year ended. Daniel was given his group certificate from the servo and went to a local accountant to get his tax return done. It was his first tax return in nearly six years. Tax returns hadn't been a high priority when he'd been a junkie and he was pleased to discover that he would be refunded nearly two grand. He began to think about what he would do with the money.

'I'm pregnant,' Naomi told him a week later. 'I didn't think I could get pregnant, I thought that years of drug abuse had ruined my body and I would never have to worry about it. Looks like I was wrong.'

But it had happened.

Daniel felt like the prison doors had just slammed shut on him.

'I need to think,' he said and walked out.

He caught a bus into the city. But in the city, he had no idea what to do. He walked around in a daze, unable to properly absorb the bombshell she had dropped on him. He thought about what fatherhood and domestic life with Naomi might be like. Try as he might, he just couldn't visualise a successful family home with her. He thought about supporting a family on his wage from the servo. Obviously that wasn't going to happen. So what were his options? The more he thought about it, the less he seemed to have.

He looked through the window of a Flight Centre store. He walked inside and saw the familiar red logo. A very nice woman with a silly neckerchief thing around her neck smiled at him, said hello, asked if she could help him.

'Umm, yeah, how much for a one-way flight to Perth?'

THE NEVER-MARRIED UNCLE

Someone ought to write a book about the funerals of lifelong bachelors, thought Andrew after they buried his uncle Clive. There is something about the death of a man who never married or had kids that is worth a book.

It had been a decent turn out in the end. Andrew and his wife Michelle, plus their kids, Auntie Katherine and a couple of people from the TAFE where Clive had been an adult education teacher for the last thirty or so years. The Pastor had been from Auntie Katherine's church, not really Clive's thing but since he'd left no clear instructions for his funeral they'd had to make executive decisions for him. The Pastor hadn't bullshitted about Clive but in being honest had made his life seem somewhat grim. "Clive Sanderson," he'd said, "was an educator, a lifelong lover of books and the arts, a somewhat solitary soul perhaps but he'd never had a bad word for anyone and had been a friend, brother and uncle to many of us here."

That was about all he could say. Uncle Clive hadn't done much with his life, at least that's what it looked like from the outside. He'd never married or had kids. Hadn't ever had a serious relationship with a woman that Andrew knew of. He'd travelled a little, gone to Europe a couple of times, but basically he'd spent his life in Adelaide living in his old house in Daw

Park that had bookshelves against nearly every wall, all bursting with books like a dam overflowing.

The big surprise came after the funeral. Clive had left his house and contents to Andrew. He was shocked when the lawyer told him. He looked over at Auntie Katherine quickly to see what she thought of it. He didn't want her to be angry, he didn't want a family drama over this. She seemed to take it placidly. Her face was unconcerned at the news.

When Andrew told his wife, she jumped for joy.

'Oh my God! That old place in Daw Park? That would be worth a fortune now, that area has gone ahead in leaps and bounds recently. It's on such a big block too, maybe we could knock it down and build units or something? Or just sell it as it is, it's an old house but it's been looked after, could get nearly four hundred grand for it without too much trouble.'

Andrew was a little startled at such naked greed. He hadn't thought that far ahead. He wasn't sure what they would do with the place but the thought of selling it for profit left a bad taste in his mouth.

They were given the keys to the place a few days later. Andrew had to sign a whole bunch of paperwork at the lawyer's office and was given an envelope with even more paperwork.

They took the kids with them when they drove to the house for the first time. The girls remembered Uncle Clive and understood he had died but being only four and six they didn't have much emotional connection to an old man they occasionally visited.

Andrew slowly turned the key in the door. Clive had died in hospital so it wasn't like there was going to be a mess or a smell here but he still thought it a little ghoulish to be entering and taking possession of a dead man's house.

The house was as Clive had left it, and as Andrew always remembered it; musty, smelling of old books. It had been set up for the comfort of a single man, no feminine touch because no woman had lived here, no dining area for entertaining guests because there had been no guests. Instead there was a supremely comfortable armchair with a footstool and a little coffee table. Rings on the table testified to all the steaming hot mugs that had rested there over the years. Andrew could see it clearly, Clive sat there stretched out with a good book and a cuppa, happy and content as any creature on God's earth.

They didn't really know where to start or what to do. They stood in the lounge room for a few minutes before Andrew stepped into the study. Michelle followed him, the girls holding her hands.

There was a great desk against one wall, just beneath the window so that whoever sat there could look out onto the front garden. The walls were hidden behind bookshelves that were nearly bursting and could not have fitted another volume in them. The desk looked noble, old and serious, made of dark hardwood and built to last forever. You could imagine Winston Churchill or a Hapsburg Emperor having a desk like this.

There was a notepad and pen in the middle of the desk, perhaps the last thing Clive had written before going into hospital. Andrew looked at the elegant handwriting. It was a poem. Andrew didn't know much about poetry, he couldn't tell if it was good or bad, original or copied. About ten lines written down. If there was meant to be more, it would never be written now, something about the birds outside calling for life while the shadows inside grow darker. He'd have to look at it again later.

For now, he directed his attention to the bookshelves. His eldest daughter Lucy stood by his side while he looked.

'Are any of these kids' books, Dad?'

'I don't think so, squirt, these are all grown up books.'

'What are they about?'

Andrew thought about the question for a minute and looked closely at the spines in front of him.

'Well, there is a lot of poetry and quite a lot of history as well, all sorts of things really. Uncle Clive was interested in lots of things, it seems.'

'Are you going to read all these books now that Uncle Clive is dead?'

'I don't know about that, sweetie, there are lots here. It would take a long time.'

'So, what are you going to do with them?'

It was a good question. There must be hundreds of books in this house, maybe even a couple of thousand, and they didn't have room at their place for them all, so what then? Charity shops? Secondhand bookshops?

'You know, if we sold them to one of those secondhand bookshops in the city as a job lot, we could get a bit of money for them.'

This was his uncle's life, they couldn't just flog it off to the highest bidder, could they? It didn't seem right although it made perfect *rational* sense.

'This was Clive's life, you know.'

'So, you're going to keep all this stuff?'

'Well, I don't know, maybe we can find some use for it. There might be some stuff we want or that the girls can have when they get older.'

Michelle raised an eyebrow and ran a finger along the nearest shelf. She pulled out a book at random.

'A history of whaling and commercial shipping in early colonial Australia 1788-1840,' she read. 'Yeah, that sounds like something we'd want to read. I'm sure the girls will be into that once they're a bit older.'

Andrew felt slightly foolish and shrugged his shoulders meekly.

'Yeah, well, we'll have a proper look through it all and maybe make up some lists of what there is before we do anything.'

Michelle took the girls out to the kitchen while he continued to potter around in the study. He could hear her opening and closing cupboard doors, the chink of crockery and the rattle of drawers. Andrew shook his head.

He sat on the carpet in the middle of the study, surrounded by books. He remembered his Uncle Clive giving him an illustrated edition of *The Hobbit* for his birthday, he must have been about eight or nine. He remembered reading it at night and having nightmares of the giant spiders in the Mirkwood.

He remembered at seventeen saying goodbye to Clive the weekend before he left for Navy basic training. Clive had a romantic view of naval life and made a lot of "our boy, the sailor" and asked Andrew to send him postcards from the exotic ports he'd imagined he would visit. As it turned out, Andrew only ever went to Darwin and Perth before being discharged on a medical after barely ten months. Andrew had felt a failure when he returned home after this short and unsuccessful Navy career. Clive had tried to cheer him up, told him that life was about trying things and if something didn't work out you just had to dust yourself off and try something else.

Clive himself hadn't tried much in life. At least not as far as Andrew could see. He'd found a comfortable role for himself at TAFE teaching adult education classes. "Second chance clubs" he called them and he'd said that most of his students had either fucked up when they were young, mostly on drugs, or had been in circumstances where education just wasn't an option. And he said he felt proud to help these people try again and make something more of their lives. He'd been a big believer in all that education-helps-society idealism. He'd been a member of something, what was it? Andrew remembered Clive showing him his membership card.

He stood up and started rifling through the drawers of the desk. He soon found it, a membership card for the Australian Democrats party dated March of 1996. Fucking thing belonged in a museum; a dead party, dead ideals and a dead man.

He looked at the card, thinking. He listened and couldn't hear Michelle and the kids anywhere.

The girls were sat on the big armchair in the lounge room looking at their Mum's tablet, some cartoon playing.

'Where did Mum go?'

'Out to the shed in the backyard. She said it's not nice for kids.'

'Okay, girls.'

He walked out the back to find her, sleeves rolled up, digging through boxes in the little shed. She looked up as he entered and he saw the sweat on her brow and the enthusiasm on her face.

'Lot of good stuff in the kitchen, like nice old china and things, might be worth a bit, plenty of stuff in here, too, this chest of drawers looks a hundred years old. Might be worth talking to some antique dealers. Have you had a look in the bedroom yet or are you still in the study?'

Andrew held his tongue for a moment.

'Yeah, still looking through the study. Are you going to look through the rest of the house?'

'Yeah, I reckon I've found everything there is to find in this shed. I'll try the main bedroom next.'

They walked back to the house in silence. Old trees cast lengthy shadows across the house and yard. Once inside they put their heads through the loungeroom door to check on the girls then went separate ways.

He sat in Clive's old chair at his desk for a moment and remembered the envelope with all the paperwork he'd been given. He'd left it on the desk when they had first come in. He opened it; it seemed to be mostly copies of all the documents he'd already signed. Then at the bottom he saw a small white envelope with his name on it.

Carefully, he opened it and unfolded the letter inside. He noted the elegant old-fashioned handwriting. His eyes focused on the page.

My Dear Nephew,

If you're reading this it means I've died. By now you've got the keys to my house and are deciding what to do with it. I'll tell you straight that I'm not particularly fussed about it. I made that house my home and had many good years there. That doesn't mean it should be kept as some sort of monument to a dead man. If you want to sell it, then sell it. If you want to live in it, then live in it. I'm dead so I have no further use for it. I left it to you because you're my only relative with young children so it seemed that you would get the most benefit from it. Do what you want with it.

I want you to know that I've enjoyed my life for the most part. I've had some good friends and good times. I know a lot of people thought I was a sad old man living alone and never getting married but that's just their opinion and we know what the opinions of other people are worth, don't we?

Now that I am nearing the end of my life, and I can look back on it, the thing I am proudest of is my work as an educator. I know some people don't think much of what I did but it gave me immense satisfaction. I helped people start their lives over again and achieve things they thought had passed them by. I may have told you this once or twice, Andrew, but most of the people in my Adult Education Classes had rough pasts. A lot of them were reformed drug addicts and alcoholics. Many had grown up in horrifically dysfunctional families full of poverty and violence.

At some point they made the decision to try again in life and they signed up for my classes. Very few of them were actually stupid but some were barely literate. Many of them had such

115

awful experiences of school as young people that they were traumatised by being in a classroom. I don't mean to boast but I had the knack of drawing these people out of their shells and engaging them in their own education. I gained a deep personal satisfaction working with my students and helping them to make something out of what was left of their lives.

If there is any great wisdom I can impart to you, Andrew, it is this simple but profound truth that I learned from those people. Life is for living and as long as you are alive there is always something that can be made of it. The key thing is to start. Start living, start turning things around, start building a better life for yourself.

My only regret in life is that I have been swimming against the tide. I am perhaps a relic of an older time with older ideals but I have always believed in rationalism, education and enlightenment. I believe in society, in educating people and helping individuals to better themselves so they can contribute to that society in a better way. I believe in fairness, justice and balance. All of these things seem to be going out of fashion now. The world around me has become colder, crueller, and even stupider. Perhaps it is for the best that I won't live to see the end result of all this. I did what I could to improve the world, I can hold my head up high. I do not know if it will make any difference in the long run.

So my life is over now, young nephew. I made what I could of it and I am at peace. You on the other hand have plenty of life ahead of you and your daughters have their whole lives ahead of them. I hope you will use whatever time is given to you wisely and you make some positive difference, however small, to the world. Life is not all about selfish pleasures. You have to give something back, contribute something to the world. I hope you will teach your girls to be good people, to care about the world around them and to treat their fellow humans with a little kindness.

So farewell, on the off chance I was wrong and there is an afterlife, then perhaps we will discuss these things at a later date. If not, then I did the best I could and that's all anyone can do.

Your affectionate Uncle,

Clive.

Andrew read it quietly and when he was finished, he placed it carefully on the desk and looked out the window. The sun was starting to fade and the green of the suburb was overtaken by shadows. For a moment he wanted to cry but he fought back the tears. Michelle was talking to the girls in the loungeroom. He heard the excited running of little feet and seconds later Lucy was by his side.

'Dad, Mum says if you say yes we can order pizza and eat it in the loungeroom and watch a Disney movie while you are sorting out Uncle Clive's stuff. Say yes, please Dad, say yes!'

He rubbed his eyes with his hands and he put his arm around Lucy, this little girl of his so full of life.

'Yeah, that'll be alright sweetie, we'll get pizza. Tell Mum to get some garlic bread as well.'

Lucy raced off to the other room shouting, 'Dad said yes and to get garlic bread!' While Andrew sat in silence at the desk, surrounded by an old man's books.

ACKNOWLEDGEMENTS

Thanks to *Flycatcher* for originally publishing 'Those Pine Trees Across the Street'.

The author wishes to thank his wife Linsey and his daughter Emily for their love and support.

The author also wishes to thank The Sundays whose album 'Reading, Writing and Arithmetic' he listened to constantly while writing these stories.

Also from Truth Serum Press by
Lewis Woolston

truthserumpress.net/catalogue/fiction/the-last-free-man-and-other-stories

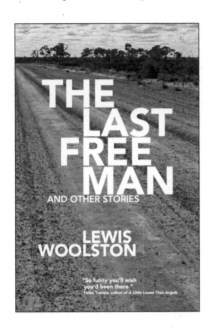

Shortlisted for 'Best Fiction' in the 2020 Chief Minister's NT Book Awards, *The Last Free Man and Other Stories* portrays characters who live in Australia's remotest areas. Many have chosen such a life, valuing independence and personal freedom above all else. Some have simply ended up there. Each story takes the reader inside the rhythms and mindset of his characters: Woolston's eye is curious and unobtrusive as he illuminates their quirks and impulses. The stories unfold with a confident sense of pace, and by the end of the collection, the reader has gained a vivid and often amusing insight into life in Australia's great outback. (*Imprint*, NT Writers' Centre)

Available in paperback and eBook.

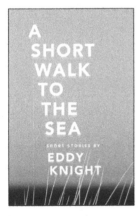